ERIC WALTERS
CATBOY

ORCA BOOK PUBLISHERS

Library and Archives Canada Cataloguing in Publication

Walters, Eric, 1957-
Catboy / Eric Walters.

Issued also in electronic format.
ISBN 978-1-55469-953-7

I. Title.
PS8595.A598C38 2011   JC813'.54   C2011-902091-2

First published in the United States, 2011
Library of Congress Control Number: 2011925029

Summary: The wild cat colony Taylor has been caring for is at risk of being
destroyed, and in order to save it, Taylor will need the help of all his friends.

*Orca Book Publishers is dedicated to preserving the environment and has printed this
book on paper certified by the Forest Stewardship Council®.*

Orca Book Publishers gratefully acknowledges the support for its publishing
programs provided by the following agencies: the Government of Canada
through the Canada Book Fund and the Canada Council for the Arts,
and the Province of British Columbia through the BC Arts Council
and the Book Publishing Tax Credit.

Design by Teresa Bubela
Cover photography by iStockphoto.com
Typeset by Nadja Penaluna

ORCA BOOK PUBLISHERS   ORCA BOOK PUBLISHERS
PO Box 5626, Stn. B   PO Box 468
Victoria, BC Canada   Custer, WA USA
v8R 6s4   98240-0468

www.orcabook.com
Printed and bound in Canada.

15 14 13 12 • 5 4 3 2

CATBOY

To all the young readers of the Toronto District School Board who contributed to the creation of the book—with a very special thanks to Jaime, who was the first to read and give feedback, and who ultimately became a character in the story.

One

I kicked the rock, and it skittered across the street and pinged off the undercarriage of a car parked on the other side of the road.

Simon laughed. "Nice shot, Taylor."

"I wasn't *trying* to hit it."

"Doesn't matter. It's not your car anyway."

He was right. It wasn't my car, just like it wasn't my house or my school or my neighborhood or my friends. Nothing was mine anymore. Nothing was the same.

"Want to hang out when we get home?" he asked.

"Don't you have homework?"

"I have to finish it before my parents get home, but that won't be till really late," he said.

Both of Simon's parents worked. They owned a convenience store, but they also had a cleaning business. Most of the time they were at the store. After hours, in the evenings and on the weekends, they cleaned shops and banks. They worked a lot.

"Before I do anything, I need to go home and get something to eat," I said. "I'm starving."

I *did* want to grab some food. I also wanted to set the table, peel some potatoes for supper and maybe tidy up and do the breakfast dishes. It made it easier for my mom when she got home. She also worked a lot and was always tired when she got home. It made her smile when I helped out.

Our move to the city had been hard for me, but I think it was harder for her. I liked to try to make her life a little easier. I didn't mind helping, but I didn't want Simon to know that was what I was going home to do. I knew there was nothing wrong with helping around the house, but I didn't know if Simon would think it was stupid or lame. I didn't have many friends, and the ones I did have hadn't been my friends for very long, so I didn't want to risk losing them.

My new school was very different from my old one, but so far I liked the differences—at least, I was learning to like them. There were twenty-seven kids in my class, and, altogether, they spoke fifteen different languages at home. I knew that because our teacher, Mr. Spence, had been talking to us about celebrating our diversity. The kids in my class were from all over the planet. After living my whole life in a little town, being in the city was like being on another planet. I was a stranger in a strange new land. One of the things that made it easier for me at my new school was that nobody was a minority, because nobody was a majority.

I was one of the few "white" kids, but that didn't matter. At my old school everybody was white, and we didn't even have an ESL—English as a second language—teacher because everyone spoke English.

My new friend Simon was Korean. Simon Park. He said Park was as common a last name in Korea as Smith was here. I didn't know anybody named Smith. He told me his parents gave him the name Simon so he'd fit in. He was born in Toronto, but he had a Korean name that he said I wouldn't be able to pronounce. He said it actually sounded like a swear word in English. That had only made me more curious, but so far he hadn't told me what it was, and he said he never would.

Simon spoke perfect English, which I guess makes sense since he was born here. He also told me he spoke perfect Korean. What did I know? He said some things to me in Korean, but he could have been counting to twelve, reciting his favorite Korean foods or just making interesting sounds.

I *did* know that he did really well in school. He told me that there were two things you had to know about Korean kids. First, their parents expected them to do really well in school. Second, no matter how well they did, it was never good enough. He told me if he ever brought home all A's, his parents would have wanted to know why they weren't all A+'s. I knew he was incredible in math. It was like the guy had swallowed a calculator.

"How about we play some basketball when we get home?" Simon asked.

"Sounds good," I said.

"You know, Taylor, you're a pretty good player," he said.

"I used to play for a rep team...you know...before."

Before. That was shorthand for "prior to our move," when we lived in a house with a basketball hoop on the driveway that had a key and a three-point line my grandfather had painted on the pavement. That was before I had to compete with other people—older kids—to play on the court behind our apartment building. The hoop had no netting, the rim was crooked and the backboard was cracked.

"Come on, this way," Simon said.

He turned down an alley that cut between some houses. Alleys made me a little nervous. There were no alleys where I came from. The only ones I knew were on shows like *CSI* and *Law and Order*. That was where the detectives usually found the body—in an alley, sort of like the one we were walking down.

I looked around. An alley really *did* seem like a good place to dump a body. There were no people but a lot of bushes, garages and the backs of stores where somebody could hide. At least it was daylight, so it wasn't that scary, just unnerving.

"This is a shortcut, Taylor. Through here," Simon said as he stopped in front of a chain-link fence. At the top was a sign that said *NO TREPASSING*. Simon pried part of the fence back.

"What's in there?" I asked.

"Like I said, it's a shortcut, through the junkyard."

I hesitated.

"Don't worry," he said. "It's only three forty-five. They don't let out the attack dogs until four."

My eyes popped open, and Simon burst into laughter. "No dogs, no worries. Everybody goes this way."

I didn't see *everybody*, just him and me. Although, him and me was a big chunk of everybody I knew.

I could see through the fence into a junkyard filled with cars and pieces of scrap metal.

"It's safe. I come here all the time," he said.

He hadn't come this way the other times we had walked home. I knew two weeks wasn't a lifetime, but still.

"Look, if you want, we can go the long way," Simon said. "It's no problem. We can walk on the street. That's the way the little kids go."

He had given me a choice, but really, he hadn't. He pulled the fence back even more to make the hole bigger. I ducked down and went through. Simon followed. I felt better having him on the same side of the fence. I'd had a strange thought that instead of coming with me, he was going to pull down the fence, trap me inside and whistle for a pack of pit bulls that would race from behind a car and—Okay, I was a little paranoid. I could trust Simon—well, at least as much as I could trust anybody I'd known for two weeks.

We threaded our way around the cars. It was pretty cool, but hadn't I seen an episode of *CSI* where they found a body in a junkyard? If alleys were scary, this place was even *more* scary.

The junkyard was big and *filled* with cars. Some were up on cinder blocks, missing wheels, while others were metal skeletons with practically everything stripped off. There were piles of cars, one on top of the other, some of them flattened to look more like metal pancakes than vehicles, while others were precariously balanced. It looked like they would all tumble over if I sneezed. I was going to avoid sneezing.

The ground, except for a few muddy patches, was covered with crushed red brick and crunched loudly under our feet.

"Aren't the owners worried about somebody stealing something?" I asked.

"I hadn't thought about that," Simon said. He stopped and unzipped his pack. "Help me put an engine in my bag."

"Yeah, right."

"It'll have to be a small one. Do you see a Mini or a VW Bug?"

"Funny. Are you saying nothing here is small enough to steal?"

"Nothing back *here*," he said. "They keep things like batteries and car radios up at the front of the yard. That's where the security guards are."

"They have security guards?" I asked, looking around anxiously.

"They don't come back here…hardly ever."

Reassuring and not reassuring all in the same sentence.

"Look, Taylor, if they chase us, just run," he added.

Even less reassuring.

"I figure if you can't outrun a security guard, you deserve to be caught," he said.

"Funny, I always thought it was best not to do anything that would cause a security guard to chase you."

A sudden movement in the shadows caught my eye. I jumped and bumped into a car.

"It's just a cat," Simon said.

A large black cat ran across our path and disappeared among the wrecks.

Simon laughed. "You're afraid of cats?"

"I'm not. It just startled me. I like cats. I *had* a cat."

"At your old place?"

"Yeah, we had to put him to sleep a year ago."

"Put to sleep? What does that mean? Did you sing him a lullaby and put little Hello Kitty jammies on him?"

"Don't be stupid."

"Stupid? Me? I wasn't the one who jumped when he saw a cat. What does *putting it to sleep* mean?"

"My cat Blinky—"

"Now that's a *stupid* name for a cat."

"I named him when I was two," I said. "What do you expect?"

"Something better than Blinky."

"Anyway, Blinky was getting old and he was sick and in pain, so we had to bring him to the veterinarian. The vet gave him a needle so he could...you know."

"So you had him killed."

"We had no choice!" I said. "He was in a lot of pain."

It had been almost a year, but I still felt bad about it. I could feel tears starting to form. Being scared by a cat wasn't nearly as bad as having Simon see me cry over one. I turned and started to walk away. Simon quickly caught up.

"I don't like cats," he said. "They're dirty."

"They're not dirty," I said, defending Blinky and all of catkind. "They wash themselves all the time."

"They wash themselves with their *tongue*," he said and made a face like he was grossed out. "But if you love cats, then this is the place to be. There are dozens and dozens of them here. I'll show you."

My desire to get out of the junkyard wasn't as strong as my curiosity. Why would there be dozens of cats here? Simon changed directions, and I trailed behind him as he wove through the rows of wrecks. Were we headed toward the front of the yard?

"There are some," he said.

Sitting among the wrecks were four cats. One was on the hood of a car, sleeping in the sun. The others were on the ground, just sitting there. The ones that were awake turned toward us. They had seen us, but they didn't move. They knew we weren't close enough or fast enough to be a threat.

"The guy who owns this place must love cats," I said.

"I don't know if he cares about them one way or another. It isn't like they're pets."

"Then what are they, *guard* cats?" I asked.

Simon laughed. "You are one funny guy. They live here. They're wild cats. It isn't like he owns them or anything."

"They live here by themselves? What do they eat?"

"I guess they catch things. You know, mice, birds, rats."

"There are rats here?"

"We're in the middle of the city. There are rats everywhere," he said. "They make their homes in abandoned cars too."

I pictured them nesting in the cushions and padding of a car. It would actually be a pretty comfortable place to live—if you were a rat.

"There are skunks and raccoons here as well," Simon said.

"Are you putting me on?"

"The city is full of animals," he said. "Go out late at night. My parents see raccoons all the time when they come home late from cleaning. Wild animals live in the parks and ravines. I've heard squirrels and raccoons get into people's attics and live there sometimes. There are animals everywhere."

"It's hard to believe."

"Why not? There are lots of things for animals to eat in the city. I've seen cats eating garbage off the streets. Sometimes kids even throw them food from their lunches."

If I hadn't eaten all of my lunch, I would have done that now.

"What about the winter?" I asked. "How do the cats survive?"

"They survive like all the other animals do. They have fur coats and they stay in their nests, or whatever you call a place where a cat goes."

"I think it's called a den or a lair," I said.

Simon slumped down, resting his back against a car. I did the same. It got us out of the sun, but, more importantly, it made us less visible if a security guard walked by. I looked around anxiously. There was nobody here but us.

A couple more cats appeared. They ambled out of the wreckage like they didn't have a care in the world. And then a fluffy white cat appeared. All four of her paws were black, so it looked as if she was wearing boots or socks. Four kittens trailed behind her. One of the other cats came over, and the kittens rubbed against it as it started to lick them. Then, out of nowhere, a piece of brick bounced in front of the cats and almost hit them before smashing against a car. The cats scattered, disappearing into the junk.

Two

I jumped to my feet and spun around. There were three guys—older, high-school aged—standing there. Judging from their expressions, they were as surprised that we were there as we were by their sudden appearance.

"What are you doing?" I demanded before I thought through what I was saying.

There was a slight delay before the first one spoke. "What do you think we're doing?" he snapped.

"You could have hit one of the cats!"

"That was the idea!" snarled the biggest of the three boys.

The other two boys were holding rocks, but he wasn't. That meant he was the one who had tossed the brick.

"You could have hurt them, or even killed one," I said.

"I didn't, but maybe our next shot will be better," he said.

Suddenly one of the other boys pulled back his arm and threw a rock. I ducked, but it soared over our heads, narrowly missed a cat and hit the trunk of a car with a thud.

"Stop it!" I screamed. "You shouldn't be throwing rocks at the cats!"

"Who should we be throwing rocks at?" the big kid asked, but it wasn't really a question. It was a threat.

"Leave the cats alone," I said, my voice cracking over the last word.

The three of them laughed. Not the response I was hoping for.

"Maybe we should be throwing the rocks at something that's easier to hit," the big guy said.

I looked around for someone to help us, but we were alone.

"Come on," Simon hissed. "Let's get out of here."

I ignored him. "Just leave the cats alone," I said again. It was more a plea than an order.

"What's it to you?" the big guy asked. Obviously he was their leader and spokesperson.

"They didn't do anything to you. They're just cats," I said.

"Shut up," Simon said out of the side of his mouth.

"Are you two going to stop us?" the big guy asked.

"Us?" Simon asked, shuffling forward. "We're just passing through. I don't even *like* cats."

I stepped forward. "I do!" I exclaimed. "And you should just leave them alone."

They started laughing again. At least I was amusing them.

"So, Catboy, what are you going to do if we don't leave them alone?" asked the big guy.

"Nothing," Simon said. "We're going to do nothing except leave."

"I wasn't talking to you!" he snapped. "I was talking to Catboy." He pointed at me.

I felt my whole body flush. What was I going to do? We were outnumbered and outsized. It wasn't as if anybody was here to take control. There were no teachers, parents, refs or adults of any kind. If they wanted to beat the heck out of us or hit *us* with rocks, there was nobody here to stop them.

"What's wrong, Catboy? Cat got your tongue?" the big guy asked, and they all burst out laughing.

I had to admit, that *was* clever. Maybe if it wasn't meant as an insult and I wasn't so scared, I would have found it funny.

Then they did something that wasn't funny at all. Two of them reached down and picked up more rocks.

"It's cruel to pick on helpless animals," I said.

"You convinced us," the big guy said.

I was shocked. Were they going to stop?

"We won't throw anything at the cats…just stupid kids," said the big guy.

I started to laugh, unexpectedly. Judging from their expressions and the look Simon gave me, everyone was confused by my laughter. I had to admit, I was confused as well. But now I was going to confuse them even more. I bent down and grabbed two rocks.

"Are you crazy?" Simon said.

"Not crazy. You need to pick up some rocks."

He didn't move.

"Now!" I ordered.

He bent down and picked up a rock.

The three of them stared at us. At least we had stunned them into silence for a few seconds. I tried to decide if it was better to fire the first rock or wait. Yes, it was better to wait.

"If we run, I think we can get back to the hole in the fence," Simon whispered. "We can still get away."

"If we run, they'll chase us or throw the rocks. Just stay here. Don't move. Don't talk."

"Good idea. If we don't move, maybe they'll forget we're here and leave," he whispered. "Maybe if we close our eyes, they won't be able to see us."

Great. Sarcasm—just what I needed. They weren't leaving, but at least nobody was throwing rocks. I glanced over my shoulder, hoping the cats had left. They were still there. In fact, *more* cats were there. I guess even cats like a good show.

"On my count, we all throw our rocks," the big guy said.

I tightened my grip on the rock in my right hand. It was a good size, a good weight. I could try to make it count.

"And we all throw at Catboy," the big guy said.

I was surprised to see Simon take a small step sideways, away from me, opening up a little space between us.

"You, Asian kid, you can leave if you want," the big guy yelled. "We only want Catboy!"

I looked at Simon. He wasn't looking at me. Was he going to take this chance to get away?

"Hurry up," the guy yelled. "Get out of here. Hop on your rickshaw and run away!"

Finally Simon moved. He bent down and grabbed another rock.

"First off, I'm Canadian, and second, they don't have rickshaws in Korea," Simon said. "What are you, some kind of idiot?"

I could almost see the guy's nostrils flair in anger. "You two aim at Catboy. The Korean kid is mine. And he's going to need a rickshaw to take him to the hospital. Throw on the count of three."

The other two boys nodded in agreement.

"One," he said.

"We throw on two," Simon said.

"Two!"

I pulled my arm back to throw, and all three of them turned and ran away, disappearing behind a pile of cars.

My mouth dropped open in shock, and I started to laugh. Simon laughed too.

"What just happened?" I asked.

"They were probably afraid because I am Korean. They might have thought I would use tae kwon do on them."

"Tae kwon what?"

"That's Korean karate," he said.

"You know tae kwon do?"

"No, but they don't know that. They see an Asian kid, and they think maybe he knows stuff like that."

I shook my head. "It has to be something else."

"What else would scare them?" Simon asked.

"Maybe they were afraid of me," a deep voice said.

I turned around. Standing right behind us, towering over us, was a security guard!

Three

I staggered backward a couple of steps, as did Simon. The guard was tall and wore a uniform, black pants and a white shirt. He had a thick beard and a bright red turban around his head. He also held a nightstick.

"We were just cutting through on our way home from school," Simon sputtered.

I was so glad he spoke, because I didn't think I could mumble out a word.

"We weren't going to take anything!" Simon exclaimed.

"Were you planning on stealing rocks?" the guard asked with a heavy accent.

We opened our hands and the rocks fell to the ground.

"Tell me your names," the guard ordered.

"I'm Simon."

"And I'm...I'm Taylor. But we weren't doing anything," I said.

"Yes, you were," he said. "You were protecting the cats."

"What?"

"I saw what happened. Those boys—those *bad* boys—were tossing rocks at the cats, and you two stopped them. You are very brave boys."

"Um...thanks," I said.

"I am Singh. Mr. Singh." He smiled, stepped forward and extended his hand in greeting.

I hesitated. Was this a trick to grab us?

"Pleased to meet you, sir," Simon said as they shook hands.

"Me too," I offered, taking his hand once I'd seen him safely release Simon's. "And thanks for saving us like that."

"You looked like you were doing well without me," Mr. Singh said.

Either he hadn't seen what was going to happen or he was being kind.

"Do you own this place?" Simon asked.

"Not me. I am only the security guard, the soldier responsible for all that is here, including the cats."

"I guess the guy who owns the place wouldn't want anybody hurting his cats," I said.

"I do not think he even knows about the cats," said Mr. Singh.

"Then they're your cats?" I asked.

He shook his head. "Nobody ever owns a cat. Ever."

"I owned a cat," I said.

He shook his head again. "No, you did not."

"Yes, I did," I protested. "His name was Blinky, and he lived in our house for eight years."

"He may have lived with you, but you did not own him. You can own a dog, but not a cat. Not any more than you can own a person or an eagle…or a tiger."

"I've heard about people owning tigers," I said. "You know, tame, trained tigers."

He smiled. "I am from India, and I know tigers. They can be in a circus, but the best a tiger will ever be is *less* wild, not really tame, only pretending to be trained until the right moment arrives when it will become a tiger once more."

"I've seen tigers that are really well behaved. Once my mother took me to a tiger show when we were in Las Vegas on holidays," I said.

Then I remembered that a few months after we'd been there, I'd read in the paper how one of the tigers almost killed its owner, the guy who had raised it from a cub.

"These cats," he said, gesturing around. "I give them food, I say nice words to them. Do you know why they do not kill me and use *me* as a meal?"

I wasn't sure if he expected an answer. It was a strange question. Cats didn't kill people.

"They do not kill me because I am bigger than them. Much bigger. If not?" He drew his finger across his throat and made a slashing sound. "Just curry-flavored kitty chow is all I would be." He paused as if he was thinking. "You boys came in through one of the holes in the fence."

"Yes," I said, feeling guilty.

"You do not need to do that anymore," he said.

"We won't," I said. "I promise."

"Me too!" Simon said.

"Good boys. Rather than coming in through one of the holes in the fence, you should come in through the front gate. I will let you in if you wish to come through the yard. You are good boys."

"Thank you," Simon said.

"Yeah, thanks."

"Now come. I will walk you to the other side. We must make sure those bad boys are gone. If they are not, I will hit them with my nightstick or maybe we will all throw rocks at them!" He laughed, and we laughed with him. "Or maybe I will pretend that I am on a cricket pitch and they are wickets!"

He made a motion like he was throwing a ball, and we laughed again. I wasn't sure what a wicket was, but I *was* sure I liked this guy.

Four

I waved a final goodbye to Mr. Singh. He waved back at us and smiled. Then he turned and disappeared among the wrecks. Thank goodness the bullies were gone, although it would have been fun to toss a couple of rocks at them.

"He's a nice guy," I said.

"Pretty nice. You should have seen your face when you turned around and saw him."

"My face? You should have seen your face! I thought you were going to wet your pants!" I exclaimed.

"Can you blame me?" he asked.

"Not really," I admitted. "He's an Arab, right?"

"He's Sikh."

"What's that?" I asked.

"They're from India."

"And they all wear those turbans?"

"Not all of them, but many do. I can't believe you don't know about Sikhs."

"There's none where I used to live."

"That's hard to believe. They're *everywhere*," he said.

"Not everywhere. Not in my town," I said.

"Well, everywhere around here."

"I've seen them around here, but I've never talked to one," I said.

"Of course you have. What about Aminder in our class?" Simon asked.

"He's Sikh?"

"Of course he is. Do you think that thing on his head is a new fashion trend?" Simon asked.

"But it's not the same as the one Mr. Singh had," I said.

"That's because he's still a boy. When Aminder gets older, he'll replace that cloth with a full turban, just like Mr. Singh's."

"I didn't know that."

"There's a lot you don't know." He shook his head. "I can't believe there are no Sikhs where you used to live. Next thing I know, you'll be telling me there are no Koreans."

I shook my head.

"None?" he said.

"There was one kid who was Chinese."

"Chinese is way different from Korean. How did you know he was Chinese?"

"He told me, and I even heard him speaking Chinese."

Simon laughed. "There's no such language as Chinese."

"Of course there is! What language do you think Chinese people speak, Japanese?"

"People from Japan speak Japanese. People from China usually speak either Cantonese or Mandarin."

"Mandarin, like the restaurant near our school?"

"Why do you think it's named that?" Simon asked.

"I hadn't really thought about it."

"Mandarin is the official language of China. There are eight hundred and fifty million people who speak it, compared to only about seventy million who speak Cantonese."

"So he was probably speaking Mandarin," I said.

"Maybe not. More Cantonese-speaking people come to North America than Mandarin, so he could have been speaking Cantonese." Simon paused. "But he could have been speaking Wu. There are more Wu speakers than Cantonese. Or even Min Nan or—"

"Are you making this stuff up?" I asked.

"Of course not. I think China has over a dozen different languages. Think about it. You're from Canada, do you speak Canadian?"

"I speak English. Just like people from England speak English and people from France speak French. Are you sure Chinese people don't speak Chinese?"

"What about Rupinder? He's from India, so does he speak Indian?" Simon asked.

I shrugged. "I don't know."

"The official languages of India are Hindi and English, but there are over twenty-two official languages in different regions across the country."

"I didn't know that. Wait, Mr. Spence was talking about that the other day, right?"

"Yeah. When he was talking about the languages we posted on the class bulletin board," Simon said.

"It's hard for me to keep it all straight. At my old school everybody just spoke English," I said.

"How boring. Remember what Mr. Spence said about Toronto being the most multicultural place in the entire world?" he asked.

"I remember," I said. "And speaking of different languages, what languages is our school newsletter in?" I asked. I didn't know what they were, but I remembered that there were four of them.

"English, of course," he said.

"That one I had figured out. What are the other three?"

"Mandarin."

"I guess I should have known that."

He laughed. "Then there's Arabic and Hindi."

"So Hindi is for Rupinder and Raj and Emal."

"Not Emal. He's from Pakistan, not India, so his family speaks Urdu."

"Would Mr. Singh from the junkyard speak Hindi?" I asked.

"Hindi and at least one other language, but maybe a couple, besides English. Most people speak two or three languages."

"I speak a little French," I said, feeling defensive.

"From what I can tell from French class, you speak *very* little French," he said.

I would have argued with him if it wasn't true.

"Okay, so let me say this in English," I said. "Thanks for standing up to those guys with me."

"What choice did I have?"

"You could have taken off when he offered to let you go," I said.

"Friends stick together."

"And you're saying you didn't at least *think* about taking him up on his offer and walking away?" I asked.

"Not a chance. There was no way I was going to *walk* away." He paused. "I was giving serious thought to *running* away, fast, like a Korean rocket, leaving behind a trail of flames like in the roadrunner cartoons."

"I'm just glad you didn't."

"There was no way I was going anywhere after that rickshaw comment. There's nothing wrong with being Chinese, or anybody else, but I hate it when people assume we're all the same. Or worse, they assume I'm not Canadian because of the way I look. I'm just as Canadian as you," he exclaimed.

I held up my hands. "No argument from me. You speak Canadian better than I do."

He laughed and gave me a slap on the back.

"That guy wasn't the brightest," I said. What I didn't say was that the first time I saw Simon, I thought he was Chinese and I was surprised by his perfect English.

"You know, you shouldn't talk about anybody not being too bright," Simon said. "You were ready to get beaten up for a bunch of stupid cats. How smart is that?"

"They needed our help," I said.

"And we almost needed the help of a team of trained doctors. Try not to do that again, at least until I become a doctor."

"You want to be a doctor?"

"I'm Korean," he said and shrugged. "I'm expected to become a doctor or a lawyer, or something with a lot of education where I can make a lot of money and make my parents proud."

"You'd be a pretty good doctor," I said.

"Thank you."

"Not that I'd ever let you take care of me, unless of course I got hit in the head with a rock or something," I said.

"Let's hope only the doctor part of that comes true."

Five

The elevator shuddered to a stop, and the door slid open. The floor of the hallway was slightly lower than the floor of the elevator.

"See you in twenty," Simon said as he stepped off.

"Make it thirty," I said.

He put a hand against the door to stop it from closing. "How about twenty-five minutes?"

"How about thirty-five? I'm really hungry."

"Okay, make it thirty. I'll meet you on the court. Bring your ball," Simon said.

"Deal."

The door skidded closed, leaving me alone. My stomach lurched as the elevator rose. I pushed the button for the eleventh floor again. The number didn't light up, just one more thing in the elevator that didn't work right. I looked over at the panel with the alarm button. If the elevator got stuck and I was trapped in here, that's what I was supposed to push.

The elevator came to a stop, and the door opened. The elevator was an inch lower than the floor of the hallway. I jumped out. I hated these elevators. They made me nervous. Simon had told me stories about people being stuck in them, sometimes for hours. That would be awful. What if you had to go to the washroom? Maybe that explained the smell in there.

This building was so different from the little house we had lived in back in our old town. There were more people in this apartment complex than there had been in our whole town. I knew my mother didn't like this building any more than I did, but it was all we could afford for now. The city was expensive. We had moved to the city so my mom could have more career opportunities. In the future she hoped to make more money, but right now things were tight.

We were really moving *back* to the city. This was where my parents had lived when I was born. Where we'd lived until I was almost two and my father had died. We moved back to the town where my mother was from so my grandparents could help her raise me.

I really missed them. I missed a whole lot about my old town.

I hurried down the hall. The carpet was worn and patched and faded. It had probably been fancy when it was first installed, twenty or thirty years ago.

As I passed each door, a rush of sounds—voices, tv, music—and smells came at me. The smells were stronger than the sounds. I didn't recognize most of them, just like I didn't understand most of the languages either. My mother had explained to me that different cultures have different foods and use different spices.

We were basically salt-and-pepper people with an occasional gust of garlic when my mother made spaghetti or lasagna or something like that. Funny, I knew those foods were from Italy, or had I read someplace that noodles were originally from China? Either way, spaghetti and lasagna seemed more Canadian than anything except for maple syrup, back bacon and beaver tails.

I pulled the key around my neck out from beneath my shirt. I fumbled with it in the lock. I always felt vulnerable, hunched at the door until the lock opened. When it clicked, I pushed open the door, stepped inside and closed the door behind me. For a second, I thought about putting the chain on the lock but decided against it. I was going out soon anyway.

"I'm home!" I called out to the empty apartment.

I knew nobody was there, but it still felt strange. When I was little, my grandfather or grandmother would be home to greet me. When I was really little, they'd walk or drive me to and from school. My grandmother always had a snack waiting for me. She'd give me a hug and ask, How was school today?

"School was fine," I said to myself. School *had* been fine today. I liked the kids in my class. I liked my teacher.

"And how was *your* day?" I asked.

She didn't answer, of course, because she was five hundred kilometers away. My mother didn't answer either, because she was halfway across the city, working at the bank. Not the branch where she worked in our town, but a bigger branch here in the city.

"I'll set the table now," I said to myself.

I hated the silence of the apartment, so I often talked to myself or turned on the tv. The tv—that was a good idea.

I went into the living room and grabbed the channel changer off the coffee table. I clicked it on. It didn't matter what was on. I just wanted background noise. I liked having company, even if it was electronic company. Even having Blinky to come home to would have made it better.

I chuckled to myself about what Mr. Singh had said. Of course I had owned Blinky. Well, in the same way Blinky had owned me.

I hurried back to the kitchen and grabbed the plates, utensils and glasses. The placemats were already on the table. I put everything out quickly. I remembered to put the fork on the left side. With only two of us, it didn't take long to set the table.

Next I grabbed a big bowl and the potato peeler from the drawer, and I opened the cupboard under the sink. That's where we kept the potatoes. I picked up the bag, and it was more than half full. We had plenty of potatoes. That was good.

Before we had moved to the city, I'd never peeled a potato or worried that we had enough potatoes or carrots or milk or bananas. It was as if they all just magically appeared on our shelves or in our fridge. Now I knew exactly what we had in the apartment and how much it cost and how much it weighed when we carried it home. I also knew when my mother got paid so we could buy more groceries. We always seemed to have everything we needed but not much more. I guess we got by.

Back home my grandparents had helped out. I knew all we had to do was ask and they'd help us now too, but Mom didn't want that. I understood.

I was looking forward to seeing them again. We planned to go back for a week at Christmas, but that seemed like a million years away.

I plopped the bowl and the bag of potatoes on the coffee table. I could watch tv while I worked.

I clicked on the Cartoon Network. *Spiderman* was on. I loved Spiderman. He was one of my favorite super-heroes. When I was a kid, I dreamed I would develop superpowers. So far, the only skill I'd managed to fully develop was the ability to peel potatoes at superhuman speed—faster than a speeding bullet! If ever there was an evil villain depriving people of potatoes, me and my peeler would be ready. I could already see the police commissioner shining a spotlight in the sky—a light shaped like a gigantic spud—to call me.

I held the peeler above my head as if it was a weapon.

The city would cheer for me. I'd be Mr. Potato Peeler! Wait, that sounds too much like Mr. Potato Head. How about Spudman? Yes, Spudman, able to overcome mounds of potatoes and—hold on, I wasn't Spudman. I was *Catboy*! Defender of cats, saving them from harm, assisted by my trusty sidekick, Simon the Korean Kid, master of tae kwon do. I'd be armed with both my potato peeler and rocks, ready to hurl them at my opponents with laser precision.

Of course, those would be our secret identities. During the day, we would be mild-mannered grade-six students. At night—well, early evening or after school—we would assume our secret identities. Actually, it might be better if I kept Simon's secret identity a secret from *him*.

The lobby buzzer squealed, and I jumped. It was probably my sidekick, the Korean Kid, wanting me to either play basketball or fight evil.

I raced over to the intercom and pushed the button. "Hello?"

"Thirty minutes is past. Are you coming down?" Simon asked.

"I'm coming."

"Bring your basketball," he said.

"For sure."

I guess that meant we were playing basketball. If it was something heroic, he would have asked me to bring the potato peeler. Speaking of which, I had almost forgotten the potatoes. I ran back to the living room, grabbed the bowl, brought it back to the kitchen and filled the bowl with water. I cleaned up the peelings and was ready to go.

Six

"Okay, everybody, let's put away our math," Mr. Spence said. "I want you to get out your reading book. It's time for silent reading."

Everybody instantly did what he said. He hardly ever needed to repeat himself. At first I thought it was because everybody was scared of him. I know *I* was scared of him at first. He was *huge*, and when he gave us the I-mean-business look, I don't think anybody, kid or adult, ever messed with him.

Simon had told me Mr. Spence used to be a professional football player. I could see that, because he *looked* like he used to play football. But I quickly discovered that kids listened to him just because.

He *could* have been scary, but he wasn't. He was really
nice. Kids did what he asked because he asked them to.
Maybe it was the way he treated us. He was an adult and
we were just kids, but he treated us with respect.

"Okay, before we begin," he said, "I want everybody
to repeat after me."

I knew what was coming next. Everybody knew.
He always did the same thing before silent reading.

"The more you read," he called out.

"The more you read!" we all said back.

"The more you know," he said.

"The more you know," we repeated.

"The more you know," he said. His voice got louder
with each phrase.

"The more you know!" we yelled back.

"The further you go!"

"The further you go!" we yelled out.

"So read, read, read!"

"So read, read, read!" we screamed.

"That's what I love!" he said. "Now get reading!"

I'd never known a teacher who was so excited about
reading or who got students so excited about it. It was
as if we were preparing for the reading Olympics.
Mr. Spence had a running total of the books we'd read.
The list ran around the walls of our classroom.

He wanted *us* to love reading because he loved

reading too. While we read, he read as well. He would sit up front, his feet up on his desk, and read. Sometimes it was a newspaper, or *Sports Illustrated*, which he said was about the best thing in the world. He also read novels— some were adult books but others were kids' novels. Sometimes he read books that students recommended to him. He also read poetry and short stories and technical sorts of journals, comic books and graphic novels. He said reading was reading; all we had to do was find something we liked.

I knew he was a teacher and trying to be a good role model for us. But I could also tell Mr. Spence simply loved to read. Then again, who didn't?

My eyes strayed up to the big posters on the bulletin board behind his desk that displayed the words for *Hello* in fifteen different languages, the same fifteen languages spoken by the kids in our class. Some were easy for me to make out, but others were written with letters or symbols that were like little pictures or strange marks. I knew one was Korean and another Chinese— no, not Chinese—Mandarin or Cantonese. There was also Cambodian, Arabic and Russian.

I tried to imagine how hard it would have been for those kids to come to this country and not speak or read English. It would have been so hard. Amazingly, they all seemed to pick it up fast. There was a kid in our class who had been in the country for less than a year, and he read almost as well as I did.

I took French, so I understood a little bit about learning a different language. But there were words that were the same in French as in English. Not just the letters of the alphabet, but words that we had borrowed from each other like *croissant*, *auto*, *café* and *pizza*. No, *pizza* was Italian.

Looking up at the words on the posters—those squiggles and symbols and little drawings—I had no idea whatsoever what some meant. It really would have been hard for kids who came from places that didn't share the same alphabet as we used.

"Taylor," Mr. Spence said.

I'd been so lost in thought, I hadn't noticed him coming over to my desk.

"Yes, sir."

"It's time for silent reading, not silent staring into space."

"I *was* reading," I said. "I was reading the posters on the wall. I was trying to figure out which languages are which."

He looked up at the posters. "That's right. We didn't say what languages they are. It should be written below. We need to fix that." He walked to the front of the class. "I'm sorry to interrupt, but Taylor has pointed out something we need to correct." He gestured to the posters. "We have proudly displayed the languages of our class, but we have failed to proudly write which languages they are. Let's take them down, one by one, and correct that."

The first poster he pulled down was a word I was pretty sure I knew. It was in Spanish. We had kids from two different countries in South America, Bolivia and Chile. I remembered that almost all of South America spoke Spanish, not Bolivian or Chilean. Brazil was one of the exceptions, where they spoke Portuguese.

"That one is mine and Agnes's," Salvador said. "That is Spanish."

I put up my hand.

"Yes, Taylor."

"Could people also say the word again so we can hear it?"

"Again, a good suggestion. You are full of good ideas today," Mr. Spence said.

Hearing him say that made me feel happy and kind of proud.

"Go ahead, Salvador and Agnes," Mr. Spence said.

"*Hola*," the two of them said together.

"Very good. Can you both say it once more, and then I'd like everybody to repeat it back to them," Mr. Spence said.

When we all repeated the word back to them together, they smiled. It was as if we'd given them something, a gift, and maybe we had.

"I'm going to write *Spanish* underneath," Mr. Spence said, "but I'm also going to write your two countries as well."

We went poster by poster, language by language, with kids saying their native *hello* and the rest of us repeating it. Some were harder for me to say than others. The words or letters just wouldn't form easily in my mouth. If that's how it was for me, was it the same for someone learning to speak English?

Each time the class answered back, it seemed to make the person happy. Even kids who were shy smiled.

"And whose is this one?" Mr. Spence asked.

"That's ours," both Jaime and Dylan said.

I looked over at Simon, and he mouthed *Mandarin* to me.

"And that is Mandarin," Mr. Spence said. "It is one of the two major languages spoken in China. The other is, of course...who has an answer?"

Hands shot up around the room, including that of Doris, who spoke Cantonese. This was fun, and it had been my idea!

Seven

On Tuesdays and Thursdays, Simon didn't walk home with me. He went to a special math class. How strange, to be as fantastic as he was at math and still go to special lessons. Then again, maybe that's why he *was* so good. In some ways he was no different than the kids who were rep basketball players and went to basketball camp every summer, or people who had a great jump shot but spent hours on the court taking shots.

I went to cross the road, hesitated, and looked around a parked truck as a car sped by only inches from my face. I staggered back. I was more aware of the traffic now, but it still unnerved me.

Both sides of the street were lined with parked cars, bumper to bumper. I didn't know how they would ever get out. There was a gap in the traffic, and I shot past several passing cars. If you waited until there were no vehicles to cross the street, you'd be waiting all day. Simon used to kid me about that—*Don't they have cars where you come from?* he'd ask—so I'd made a point of walking more "city." Back home the drivers looked out for people crossing the road, especially around schools. They'd slow down and sometimes even stop and wave you across. Here in the city, it was as if the drivers got bonus points for close calls with pedestrians.

Where I grew up, there were cars and pickup trucks, but not much else. Here there were so many cars and trucks, big and little, as well as lots of bikes, mopeds and motorcycles. A bus line connected to the subway that ran alongside the main roads. The only public transit system in our old town was a local taxi— Bert's Taxi.

I knew Toronto wasn't that far from our old town, but it was so different, it was as if I was in a different country. In my old town there were houses, of course, but nothing like here. There were a lot more of them here, but there were so many different styles. There were singles, attached and row houses, and they were all painted different colors and in different states of repair. Some were neat and tidy with perfect lawns and flowers. Others looked like they were abandoned. In between the houses were stores, offices, apartments and factories, all stuffed together like a crazy patchwork quilt. And in the city there were people, lots and lots of people everywhere. Our old downtown had been a few stores, the Legion, the arena and the beer store.

I'd been thinking about heading through the hole in the junkyard fence, but I was worried about running into those bullies. Even Catboy didn't want to face those evildoers without the assistance of the Korean Kid. But I did want to see the cats.

I changed direction and headed toward the main gate. I could find Mr. Singh and take him up on his offer to go in through the front.

I approached the fence surrounding the junkyard. A canvas covering over the fence blocked what was on the other side, but I could see the cars—a mess of wrecks and parts strewn about—through some large rips and tears.

There was a little guardhouse beside the fence, and towering over it was a gigantic billboard. It showed a big, shiny-new building and the words *COMING SOON—CONDOS—LIVE THE CALIFORNIAN WAY!*

I'd seen enough tv shows set in California to know that there was nothing about that building that looked

Californian. But, hold on a second, did that mean the junkyard was becoming condos?

"Hello, my friend!"

I looked over. It was Mr. Singh. I waved, and he walked out of the guardhouse toward me.

"Are they building condos here?"

"Yes, coming soon," he said. "That is what the sign said when it was put up *three* years ago. It is now an old sign, and there are no condos planned, so maybe we should not always believe what is written."

"Oh, that's good."

"I am sure it will happen one day though," he said. "Nothing stays the same."

I knew that.

"This neighborhood was for working people, regular people, but now the land is too valuable to stay a junkyard forever. I sit here and watch things. I guess that is what a security guard is supposed to do. But I also think about what I see. I have seen the stores on the street changing," he said. "The dollar stores and instant loan places and Laundromats are being replaced."

"They are? There's still a dollar store."

"There used to be three. Two are gone. One became a yoga studio, and the other is a place serving four-dollar cups of coffee. Can you imagine *any* cup of coffee in the world worth *four* dollars?" He laughed. "What are they doing, serving it in a cup made of gold?"

I shook my head in agreement. I liked listening to him talk. It wasn't only the things he said, but the way he said them. There was a sort of rhythm to his words that was musical.

"You know the condos are not far behind when the dollar stores start becoming yoga studios, art galleries and doggie bakeries," Mr. Singh said.

"Doggie bakeries?"

He laughed. "There is one a few blocks away. It makes treats for people's pet dogs. Some people have more money than they know what to do with. Well, it is their money. The condos will come."

"But not now," I said.

"Not yet, but ultimately this whole city will become one gigantic condo development. There will be no room for factories, or businesses like this scrapyard."

"I guess that's too bad."

He shrugged. "I will get another job. Maybe I will guard the condos instead. Are you here to say hello or to take a shortcut?"

"Can I do both?"

"Of course. Come, I will walk through with you. It is time for my rounds."

"Your rounds?" I asked.

"A bad guard sits in his little house and reads the paper. A good guard walks around the property every hour. I am a good guard. I was on one of my rounds when I found you and those bad boys."

He pushed the large metal gate, and it opened with a long, loud groan. I stepped inside, and he closed the gate behind us.

"So you think I could stop and see the cats, right?" I asked. "I saved them a bit of my lunch."

"Of course." He paused and then chuckled. "I saved them a bit of mine too," he said quietly. He looked like a guilty little boy.

He popped into his guardhouse and returned holding a paper bag.

"I have a bit of my baloney sandwich. Do you think they like baloney?" I asked.

"They like everything! We have a saying: beggars cannot be choosers. Come, we will find the cats."

I followed as he led me through the yard. I tried to figure out the layout, but one row of wrecks looked like all the others.

"Taylor, what grade are you in?" Mr. Singh asked.

"Grade six."

"And do you have brothers and sisters?"

"Just me. Do you have kids?" I asked.

"I have four children, but they are older than you. Two of my children are in university and two are finished their schooling. My oldest son is a doctor, and my oldest daughter is a chartered accountant."

"That's great! You must be so proud of them."

"I am proud of all my children, such good children they are. My littlest girl is training to be a teacher—perhaps she will be your teacher some day. And my youngest, another boy, he wishes to follow in my path."

"He wants to become a security guard?" I blurted out.

"No, no, no," he said with a laugh. "He will become a lawyer. In Canada I am a security guard. In India I was a lawyer. I worked for a very big firm, very important."

"But if you were a lawyer there, how come you aren't a lawyer here?"

"Rules, rules and more rules. There are many people from other countries who cannot become qualified to practice their professions in this country. There are doctors from other countries driving taxi cabs in Canada."

"But that doesn't make any sense. We need doctors and lawyers."

"It does not need to make sense, it simply is," he said. "But in fairness, they told me before I immigrated

I would probably not be able to practice law without going back to school. With a family to raise, there was not the money for that, so I am a proud soldier, a security guard."

"That must have been hard to come here knowing you'd have to stop being a lawyer."

"It was hard, but it was the right decision for my children and their futures. My oldest boy, my doctor son, wants me to stay at home and he will support me. I tell him that I am still the father, and if *he* needs money, he can come to *me*. I will give him some money!"

Mr. Singh sounded so proud. "There were many things that were hard in coming here. I knew very little English," he said.

"You speak so well now."

"I learned. There was so much new to learn, but the hardest adjustment was the weather. It is very *cold* in this country, and who knew winter could be so long!"

"It's not nearly as cold here as where I come from."

"You are not Canadian?" he asked.

"I am, but I'm from a town up north. Up there, they have snow before Halloween and it stays until the end of March, or later."

"You must be from the North Pole!" he said and started to laugh.

"Not quite, but farther north than here," I said.

"There is one good thing about a Sikh coming to this country. We come equipped for the cold," he said, pointing up to his bright red turban. "I like to think of this as my Sikh tuque. At least my head is warm in the winter!"

He smiled broadly, and I did too.

"How long have you been in Canada?" I asked.

"Twenty-one years. I have been a Canadian citizen for almost fifteen years. Two of my children are born citizens and the other two became Canadians as soon as possible. You know that sometimes people ask me, *Where are you from?* and I tell them Toronto. Then I tell them about where I was born. I am proud to be Sikh. But I am also proud to be Canadian. You must always take pride in where you come from, but also in where you are and where you will be in the future."

"I guess I never thought about it. I was born here," I said.

"Like my two youngest."

"And so were my parents and their parents."

"And before that?" he asked.

"My great-grandparents on both sides were from Scotland."

"Be proud of your heritage. But, in this country, we are almost all immigrants. Some find it more difficult to be here than others. Most of their difficulties aren't in where they are but what they bring with them."

"I don't understand," I said. "You mean like money?"

"Money is one thing that would make life easier, but I am talking about an attitude. I will tell you a story," he said. "My wife says I like telling stories too much, that I should be a writer and not a lawyer or a security guard." He paused. "Not that I am saying anything bad about my wife. She is a very good woman, but here is the story.

"A man moves to a new country. He wishes to know what the people are like in this new place, so he goes to see the king and asks him. The king, instead of answering, asks the man one question, 'What were the people like where you came from?' The man replies, 'They were kind and generous.' The king says, 'That is how you will find them here.'

"A second man moves to the country, and he too goes and sees the king and asks the very same question about the people, and the king, in turn, asks him about the people in the country he left. The second man answers that the people where he came from were mean and unfriendly. The king replies, 'That is how you will find them here.'

"Do you understand my story?" Mr. Singh asked.

"I think so. It's sort of like who you are and what you're like will be a big part of what happens for you wherever you live."

"Exactly!" he exclaimed, and he gave me a big pat on the back. "No country is perfect. Here, like everywhere else, there are good people and bad people. Some of those bad people will only look at this," he said, tapping a finger against his skin. "Or this," he said, gesturing to his turban. "Instead of looking at the person." He paused. "But in this country at least we *know* we are supposed to treat each other as equals. Here, in this country, a security guard can raise children who can become doctors and lawyers and teachers."

"Or the prime minister," I said.

"Or the prime minister. We Sikhs love politics. You mark my words, there will be a Sikh prime minister someday. But for today, I will be a proud Sikh soldier, and here are the cats I guard!"

Eight

There were at least a dozen cats standing, walking around, sitting or curled into balls sleeping, either on the ground or on the roofs or trunks of the wrecked cars.

"There are a lot of them," I said. "How many do you think there are altogether?"

"I am not certain, and the number changes all the time."

"I saw some kittens," I said. "And some teenager-sized cats."

"Yes, kittens are born all the time, and other cats disappear or die. I find the remains sometimes."

"Do they just get old?"

"I do not believe that many live long enough to die of old age. It is not an easy life. There are many things: often cars or trucks on the street, sometimes dogs get in the yard through the holes, and of course people, like those bad boys or even worse."

"What could be worse?" I asked.

"Poison."

"People poison them? That's awful!"

"I think sometimes it is done on purpose. They give them poisoned food. And other times it is by accident."

"How do you *accidentally* poison something?" I asked.

"They are trying to poison the rats, and the cats either eat the poison or they eat the poisoned rat." He shook his head slowly and his expression was sad. "I have seen it. It is such a terrible way to die. Much pain."

I didn't want to think about that.

"At least they are mostly safe in here," he said. "Especially now that the yard is not being worked in very much. The owner, the man who ran the yard, he got very old and could not do it anymore. His son, he is not interested in the business, only in selling the land. Before, there were always trucks and forklifts. Sometimes they would run over the cats, or they were crushed when the wrecks were moved. But now the yard is mostly quiet. They are waiting for the condos to come."

"I'm glad it's better for the cats now."

"It is better, but still not easy, especially in the winter. It is not just some Sikhs who do not like the cold."

"At least they have fur coats."

"That is not enough. See the one cat, the black and white one," Mr. Singh said, pointing.

"Half of them are black and white."

"On the car, the blue car. You see how he is missing part of one ear?"

"Yeah, I see."

"Frostbite. Some even freeze to death. Some are not well fed and suffer from diseases, and the winter finishes them off."

"Don't they have places to get out of the cold?"

"Some nest in the wrecks or in holes in the ground."

"I didn't know cats dug holes like that," I said.

"I do not believe they dig holes. They simply use holes dug by other animals or ones naturally formed. Some of those holes are very, very deep. Some people even leave blankets for them. I come in and find the cats lying on them, but cats do not know how to bring those into their burrows."

It was good to know some people cared enough to try to help the cats and not everybody was tossing rocks or spreading poison.

"Sometimes it is not just me who feeds them. I find cans of cat food on the ground sometimes," he said.

"That's nice."

"It would be nicer if they did not leave the cans as garbage. This is a junkyard not a garbage pit," he said. "Look, do you see that?" A big black cat ambled into view. On his forehead was a burst of white that looked like a star. "See what he has!"

In his mouth was either a large mouse or a small rat.

"That one is a good hunter! I've seen him often with something that he has caught. Mice or rats or birds and pigeons. He helps to keep the yard free of such things."

"Does he share with the other cats?" I asked.

"I think with his mate, and perhaps some scraps with the others. There are some cats who would simply take his food. You see that big one over there? He is not nice and takes what he wants."

A big tabby cat—a *really* big tabby cat—had come out from under a car. On cue, the other cat, the mouse still in his mouth, scurried off in the opposite direction, quickly disappearing from view.

"If there was a king of this colony, that would be him," Mr. Singh said.

"If he's like the king, what advice would he give to a new cat who asked about the cats in this colony?" I asked.

"His advice would be short and sweet, especially if it was another male cat. He would swat him on the head and send him on his way. Cats do not like new cats. They get into tremendous fights," Mr. Singh said. "Before, when I did the night shift, I could be startled right out of my shoes. It would sound like someone was being killed, and I guess they practically were."

"There's a night shift here?" I asked.

"Always a guard, but not necessarily a good guard. Some just listen to the radio or read the paper or go to sleep. That is not how to do your job. You must take pride in whatever you do, whether it is being a doctor or a lawyer or a humble security guard."

"But now you don't work nights, do you?"

"I am senior. I only work days, no nights or weekends," he said.

"So maybe it's better if I don't come here in the evenings or on the weekends in case the other guards get angry or chase me away," I said.

"No one will be angry. I will tell them that you are my friend, and they will leave you alone. I am the *senior* soldier, and they listen to me."

"Thanks. I was just wondering, why doesn't somebody just fix the holes in the fence so people can't come in?"

"We used to fix them. By the next day they'd be cut open again, so there was no point. Better to just leave them alone," he said. "But now, let us feed the cats."

This was what I'd been waiting for.

"Move slowly, so they do not run away," he instructed.

Very slowly we approached the cats. Those that were sleeping woke up and quickly got to their feet, ready to flee. A couple of the smaller cats retreated, and some disappeared beneath the wrecks.

But not the big tabby, the king cat. He remained motionless but looked at us suspiciously. He looked like he had nothing to fear from us, and judging from his size, maybe he was right.

"Throw your food to the king first," Mr. Singh said.

I undid the zipper of my bag to get the sandwich. The cats reacted to the sound of the zipper, becoming more alert, more aware and more wary.

The big cat came forward a few feet. He was still a safe distance away but closer than the others. He stood directly *between* us and the other cats. His stare became a hard glare, and his tail swished back and forth. With a dog, that's a good sign. With a cat, it isn't.

"It looks like he's guarding them," I said. "Protecting them from us."

"I think he just wishes to be first in line for dinner. I am sure he can smell the food in your hand, even if he cannot see it clearly."

I tore off a little piece of the sandwich—bread and baloney. I hadn't eaten any of it. I wasn't a big fan of baloney. I tossed it toward him. He bounded forward and with one paw batted it out of the air and onto the ground. He pounced on it like it was alive!

"Now that he is occupied, we can feed the others," Mr. Singh said.

He dug into his bag and removed a piece of bread. He ripped it into small pieces and tossed it at the cats. They scrambled, either after pieces or to run away. I quickly divided my sandwich and did the same, causing another little stampede.

As if a dinner bell was ringing, other cats came out. There were more than twenty of them feeding and fighting over the bits of food. The black cat, the hunter, didn't come out, because he didn't need my leftover tidbits. He had taken care of himself.

"Have you given any of them names?" I asked.

"No names. There are too many, and they come and go. Many look the same," Mr. Singh explained.

"Would it be all right if I named some of them?"

"You can name them all if you wish. Just do not expect them to come when you call them."

The big tabby walked toward three cats scrapping over a couple of remaining tidbits. Two of them saw him coming and scrambled away. The third didn't and received a swat to the head. The cat tumbled over and scurried away.

"He's not very nice," I said.

"He does not need to be nice. He is the king."

"Like Scar from *The Lion King*." I tried to explain, "It's a movie, a Disney movie. It's really good. Do you know *The Lion King*?"

Mr. Singh started singing "The Circle of Life" from *The Lion King*. He was off-key but knew the words. I couldn't help but smile. "Who does *not* know *Lion King*?" he asked. "That Scar was a very *bad* leader, but it was a very *good* movie."

"Does anybody ever come here to adopt one of the cats, to make it a pet?" I asked.

"Oh, no, never. That would not be possible."

"Why not?"

"These cats are not pets. They are too wild," he said.

"What about if somebody took a kitten?"

"When they are very little, they need to be with their mother to survive. When they are older, they are already too wild. They can never be pets. Never."

I knew he was right, but still.

Nine

I put up a shot and it bounced off the rim. Simon, who was short but like a bulldog, grabbed the rebound and put it back up for a basket. That was game.

"Good game," Devon said as he gave Simon a slap on the back.

We tapped hands with both Alexander and Devon. They were good losers, and we were good winners. No point in being jerks about it or trash talking. They were just as likely to win the next game as us. Besides, when you put down the people you play against, you're just putting yourself down as well.

"Taylor!"

My mom was walking toward us, smiling and waving. I looked at my watch. I'd lost track of the time because I was so preoccupied with the game. I should have gone up and done a little bit more work around the apartment, but still, it was in pretty good shape.

"Hey, Taylor's mom," Simon said.

"Hello, Taylor's friend, Simon," she said. "And Taylor's other friends, Devon and Alexander."

I could tell she liked my new friends and was particularly fond of Simon. But why wouldn't she like them? They were polite guys and worked hard at school.

I knew she'd been worried about the new friends I would make, and my grandparents had been worried even more. I guess when all you know about Toronto is what appears on the nightly news, you could get the impression a lot of bad things happen here. But none of that stuff happened at my school or in my building.

"I was just heading up to the apartment," I said.

"Stay if you want, and I'll get supper on the table."

"The potatoes are peeled and sitting in water," I said.

I had discovered I didn't have to hide the fact that I helped my mom out, because the other guys all helped around their places too.

"You are such a sweetheart. And those will go very well with what I have right here."

She held up one of the plastic bags she was carrying. Peeking out the top was a KFC box!

"I thought I smelled something special," I said, but what I thought was, Do we have enough money for that?

"This is a special meal for a special celebration," she said. "Or at least a potential celebration."

"What are we celebrating?" I asked.

"Yeah, what are we celebrating?" Simon added. "And by the way, if you need somebody else to do the celebration eating, I could be persuaded to eat some KFC."

"Count me in too!" Devon exclaimed.

"And me," Alexander added.

"You are all most welcome to join us for a meal, another time. Tonight I only bought enough for two."

"So what are we celebrating?" I asked.

"Technically, nothing yet. I have to discuss it with you first," she said.

"With me?" Now I was equal parts curious and worried. "What is it?"

"Nothing bad, so don't worry. Let's talk about it over dinner."

"In that case, we should go straight upstairs and eat. I'm hungry," I said.

"Hungry or curious?" she asked.

"Can't somebody be both?"

"Then let's go," she agreed.

I said my goodbyes to the guys and we started off.

"Sure you don't want me along?" Simon yelled. "I don't eat much!"

My mother laughed, and it made me smile. I took one of the bags from her.

"How was school today?" she asked.

"Not bad. Actually it was *muy bien*. At least, that's what I'd say if I was talking to somebody who was Spanish," I said.

"*Très bien* is what I'd say back to somebody who was French," she said.

"Mr. Spence likes when we try different languages."

My mother went to put her key in the lobby door of our apartment building, but I pulled it open.

"It's busted again," I said.

"So much for security. Would it be too much to ask that we could have that fixed? But enough complaining. So this Mr. Spence seems like a pretty good teacher," she said.

"He's pretty cool. Do you know any Gaelic?" I asked.

"Gaelic? Where is that coming from?"

"From our heritage. I'd like to add Gaelic to our heritage wall in the class."

"I'll see what I can do. Have you tried the Internet?" she asked.

"Not yet. I thought I'd try the Inter-mom first."

We stopped at the elevator. Somebody had added more graffiti to the wall. My mother shook her head. I knew what she thought about that.

"Devon really doesn't like the graffiti either," I said. "He thinks they should kick people out of the building for doing things like that."

"Devon is a smart boy."

"He says it's disrespectful to everybody in the building," I said.

The elevator door opened to our floor, one inch too low. We stepped up to the corridor.

"That's nice you're getting to know new people, especially so many nice people," she said.

She unlocked the door to our apartment, and we stepped inside.

"So what's the news?" I asked.

"Let's wait until dinner, when we can have a sit-down discussion."

"Let's not. You can't start telling me something and then stop and make me wait. That's not fair."

She nodded her head. "You're right. I'll tell you. I was offered a promotion at work today."

"That's wonderful!" I gave her a big hug.

"It's more responsibility and more money. Not a fortune, but a nice little raise."

"That's even better. To get a promotion after only being there three months is really something," I said.

She laughed. "Sometimes you act as if you're the parent. I told my boss I'd let him know my decision tomorrow."

"What's to decide? Don't you want the job?"

"That's what we have to discuss. The promotion means I'll be working two evenings a week and every second Saturday morning."

"So?"

"So, I'm not sure I should be leaving you alone more than I already do. It's not fair to you."

"Look, I'm not a baby. There's nothing to discuss. Didn't we move here so you could have a job with more chances of a promotion?"

"Well…"

"Then wouldn't it be crazy for you not to take the job?" I asked.

She smiled.

"Take the job. We can use the money, and you deserve the promotion."

She looked at me thoughtfully. "How old are you again?"

"Twenty-seven on my next birthday," I said with a grin. "And that makes me old enough to know what the right thing to do is. Tell them tomorrow that you'll take the job."

"Okay, I'll tell them and—" She stopped as she saw that the table was already set. "Thank you. That is very considerate."

"Don't I always set the table?" I asked.

"You do, but it's still considerate, still appreciated and still worth thanking you for," she said.

I followed her into the kitchen and pulled the KFC box out of one of the bags. There was another box underneath. I pulled it out as well.

I thought about what she'd said to the guys about only having enough chicken for the two of us.

"How much chicken did you get?" I asked.

"I bought enough for the two of us, and I got some more for your friends."

"For my friends? But you said you didn't have enough for them, and they couldn't have dinner with us."

"Not *those* friends."

She opened up the bigger of the two boxes. It had bones and French fries and some buns. "For your cat friends."

"Thanks so much!"

"That stuff was in their garbage. The guy behind the counter at KFC thought I was either a little crazy in the head or trying to get some free food."

"The cats are going to *love* it."

"I know those cats are important to you. You've spent a lot of time talking about them over the past couple of months," she said.

"I guess I do talk about them a lot," I said.

"I also know you still miss Blinky. I miss him too. Maybe someday we can get you another cat."

"I already have about forty cats." I paused. "But thanks, really. Someday that would be nice."

"Are you sure?"

"I'm sure," I said. "Besides, isn't this building a 'no pets allowed' place?"

"I'm sure there are a few cats in here, but you're probably right. It would be better if we didn't have a pet, at least for now."

Ten

"Okay, we only have a few minutes before the bell goes," Mr. Spence said, "so there's just enough time for a review."

We'd spent a big chunk of the afternoon studying the United Nations.

"Who can tell me when the UN was founded?"

Two dozen hands went up, including mine. He nodded to Mohammad.

"Nineteen forty-five," Mohammad said.

"Correct. And now, which city, so nice it was named twice, is the home to the United Nations?"

Every hand went up again.

"Rupinder?"

"New York, New York, in the United States," Rupinder answered.

"Correct again. It's a great city. How many people have been to New York?"

This time only two hands were raised. I thought it would be incredibly cool to go to New York. I could hardly imagine a place bigger and busier than Toronto, but I knew New York was *way* bigger.

"When you get older, you should all try to see that city. Remember, travel is a great education," Mr. Spence said. "How many member states are there in the UN?"

Almost every hand went up.

"Simon?"

"One hundred and ninety-two countries have official status," Simon said.

"Another correct answer, although some people have difficulty believing there are that many countries in the world. But I invite them to visit Toronto, where you can find people from every one of those countries living here."

"And maybe all in the same class," Simon said, and everybody laughed.

"That would be one incredibly big class," Mr. Spence added. "But one I'd love to teach. Now back to the review. How many of those one hundred and ninety-two countries make up the Security Council?"

Several hands shot up. I knew the Security Council was made up of the biggest or most powerful countries. The permanent members had the power to "veto" any vote, which meant if all the other countries wanted something and one of those countries didn't, then it didn't happen.

"Alexander, can you answer that, please," Mr. Spence said.

I turned around. Alexander had his head buried in a book, no surprise. He read more than anybody I'd ever met.

"There are five permanent members of the Security Council," Alexander said without raising his eyes. "They are the United States, Russia, England, France and China. There are also ten other members, who are elected to a two-year term on a rotating basis by the other member states."

"Very good. Not only did Alexander answer that question correctly, but he also answered my next two questions, and all without losing his place in the book he's reading." Mr. Spence paused. "Alexander, have you been peeking at my notes?"

Alexander looked up from his book in surprise. "No, sir, I would never ever look at your—"

"Alexander, I'm just joking. Great answers. Next question. What functions does the United Nations perform?"

A series of short answers were given, including signing treaties, deciding on international laws, settling disputes, dealing with emergencies like earthquakes and floods, planning for the future and taking action on global issues like pollution, the oceans and the Antarctic.

"Those are all great answers. Now my final question. What is the purpose of the United Nations? Why does it exist? And please, I don't want anybody to repeat its function."

For the first time, there weren't any volunteers to answer the question. Lots of kids liked to answer questions that had a right or wrong answer, especially if they knew they had the right answer. Me, I liked when an answer couldn't be right or wrong. I raised my hand.

"Taylor."

Now I had to think through my answer.

"I think the world is like this classroom," I said. "We have people from all over the world, from different countries and cultures, who speak different languages."

"We do have a world within these walls," Mr. Spence agreed.

"And the same way we've been learning about our differences and how to say hello in each other's languages, we've also been learning about how we're all the same, and we all have the same rights. We have our classroom rules," I said, gesturing to the big chart hanging on the wall that we made up that first day of school. "The United Nations is just a big way of helping us all get along together, peacefully and respectfully, and happily solving whatever problems we might have."

Mr. Spence didn't answer right away. He had a thoughtful look on his face. "And that, class, is *not* a good answer."

My heart dropped.

"That," he said, "was a *great* answer."

He started clapping and the rest of the class joined in. I felt myself start to blush.

"I'm starting to wonder if both you *and* Alexander have been looking at my notes," he said.

"Mr. Spence," Simon said, "we all talked about where we're from, but you didn't tell us where your family is from."

"I was born in England."

"But you don't talk with an accent," Simon noted.

"Of course I do. Everybody talks with an accent. I just happen to talk with a Canadian accent because I moved here when I was young."

"So you're Canadian," Rupinder said.

"I'm a proud Canadian, born in England, whose parents were from Jamaica, just like Sally and Devon's families are from Jamaica."

The bell rang, and people started to rustle.

"Please remember to read tonight and do your journal entries," Mr. Spence said. "Class dismissed!"

Everybody got to their feet. I was anxious to get moving. Not only was I going to be feeding the cats the KFC my mother had gotten, but I wasn't going alone. Simon and I had been talking so much about the cats that a few of the other kids had asked if they could come along. So Mohammad, Alexander, Rupinder, Devon and Jaime were going to come with us. Initially I wondered if Jaime, being the only girl, would be uncomfortable. But then I remembered she played soccer with us at recess and handled herself well around the guys. She didn't take any "guff" from people, whether they were male or female.

Mr. Spence wandered over to where Simon and I were getting our stuff together at the back.

"I think I'm going a bit crazy," Mr. Spence said. "I couldn't stop thinking about chicken all day."

"I guess that's my fault," I admitted reluctantly. I unzipped my backpack, and before I removed the box, the smell wafted out. I pulled the carton partway out.

"You had KFC for lunch?" he said.

"It wasn't for me, and it's not really a lunch. It's just bits and pieces. It's for the cats." I quickly explained about the cat colony.

"That's very nice, but are you sure you should be going in the junkyard?" Mr. Spence asked.

"My mother knows about it," I said. "She was the one who got me the scraps from KFC."

"And we go in with Mr. Singh," Simon added. "He runs the place, and he says he likes us there."

"Well, as long as your parents know," he said. Mr. Spence took a deep breath. "I'm definitely having KFC tonight."

"We have KFC every night at my place," Simon said.

"You do?" Mr. Spence and I said in unison.

"Sure. KFC, Korean food and chow."

Eleven

"Are you really, really sure we should be doing this?" Mohammad asked.

"It's okay. We're allowed," I said.

"If I get in trouble, my parents will be really upset with me," he said.

"Mo, we're going to feed some cats, not rob a bank," Simon offered.

"Mohammad, we're okay," I said. "We're going in through the front gate. The security guard, Mr. Singh, will let us in. It's all good, okay, buddy?"

"Well, okay," said Mohammad.

While it would have been quicker to cut through the hole in the fence, I wanted everybody to meet

Mr. Singh, and I wanted him to meet them.

We were a strange little posse. There was Simon from Korea, Mohammad from Somalia, Jaime from China, Rupinder from India, Devon from Jamaica, and Alexander from Russia. And if you wanted to go back far enough, I was from Scotland. Then again, if you went *really* far back, we were all probably from Africa.

We were like a slice of the United Nations. We were from all over the world, and we were all friends.

Mr. Singh was in his booth. He saw us coming, gave us a big wave and a big smile. I'd already talked to him about bringing some people with me, so he was expecting us.

"Good day, my friends!" he called out.

I introduced him to everyone. He greeted them all and said something to Rupinder in one language and something to Mohammad in another language. That made them both smile.

"How many languages do you speak?" I asked.

"Five languages very well, but it is always wise to know how to offer a brief greeting in many languages, such as Arabic."

That was good advice. Even my awkward attempts to say hello to people based on the class posters made people smile or laugh politely.

It didn't surprise me that Mr. Singh spoke several languages, and I wasn't surprised at the way he greeted everybody. He was friendly and respectful to everyone. Even though he was an adult and we were just kids, he didn't *treat* us like kids.

He reminded me of Mr. Spence. Mr. Singh would have been a good teacher too.

"We brought food for the cats," Simon said.

"All of us," Devon said. "I hope they like patties."

"And samosas," Rupinder added.

"Who does not like those things?" Mr. Singh asked. "I am thinking the cats are eating better than the security guard. I am going to have to fight them for the scraps!"

He swung the gate open, and we entered the yard. Devon and Jaime had been here before, but it was the first time for the others. I remembered how nervous I'd been the first time I came to the junkyard with Simon. It seemed so long ago, but really it had only been less than two months. I had been visiting the cats so much since then, it seemed longer than that. Mr. Singh had joked that he should either start charging me rent or paying me a wage as a security guard. And in some ways I did feel like a security guard. Not for the yard, but for my cats. *My* cats—they did feel like mine. I didn't own them, but I felt responsible for them.

"Do I smell chicken?" Mr. Singh asked.

"You have a very good nose," I said.

"Not as good as the cats. I have read that cats can smell twenty times as well as humans, so I am sure they already know you are here."

Mr. Singh stood back, letting me lead the way. I was sure he was doing it so I could be the leader with my friends.

We approached the cat colony.

"Let Taylor go first," Simon said.

"Yeah, he should," Jaime agreed. "You'll see why."

The others stopped, and I kept walking. It *was* better if it was only me at first. I entered the center of the colony, or as I'd started calling it, the Town Square. There were already more than a dozen cats waiting. I was expecting them to be there, and they were expecting me.

I recognized many of them. Kittens and mothers, teenagers, full-grown tabbies and toms, and, of course, sitting on his throne—a blue Buick—in the very middle was King.

I walked slowly, trying to be graceful like a cat. My feet skimmed slightly above the ground as I tried to keep my footfalls soft and quiet—at least quiet to human ears, but probably loud to them. I looked around without gazing directly at any specific cat. They didn't like to be stared at, especially if they were looking directly at me.

The cats allowed me to enter their kingdom. None of them ran from me. I edged forward even slower, an inch or two at a time.

A rock—a big gray rock that shone against the sea of crushed red brick chips—marked the closest I'd ever been. Each day I'd been able to move it forward another inch or two. I put my toe against it and nudged it forward. I was closer to them than ever before. It was a new world record for Catboy! Perhaps I had developed the superpower to be temporarily invisible. Invisibility *and* a potato peeler would be a great combination!

Then I whistled. It was neither melodic nor loud, but it was enough for them to hear, and it was familiar to the cats. Their ears perked up, and more cats came out of the wrecks and into view. Many of them I recognized. I knew them by their appearance, but I also knew their behaviors and personalities. I scanned the crowd looking for my favorites.

"That's amazing," I heard Mohammad say behind me.

"It's like they know him," Devon said.

"They *do* know him," Simon said. "Can we come closer now?"

"Hang on," I said.

I slowly removed my pack. The sound of the zipper opening caused the cats to freeze.

I removed the box of chicken pieces and opened it. The smell was strong, even to me.

I tossed the first piece, the biggest piece of meat, to King. He pounced on it. It wasn't that I thought he deserved it, or that I wanted to give it to him, but if I didn't, he would chase away and swat at the cat that got the first piece. He didn't care if it was another tomcat or a mother cat or even a kitten. Getting between him and whatever he wanted wasn't wise. I *really* didn't like him.

I scattered bones, buns and pieces of meat on the ground for the others, and they started eating.

"You can come now," I said. "Just be slow and quiet."

Everybody had saved bits of their lunches, and the cats were soon treated to an international feast. It was obvious the cats were enjoying the meal almost as much as we were enjoying feeding them.

"See that one there," I said, "the white cat with the black feet? I call her Miss Mittens. You can probably tell which of the kittens are hers."

She had four kittens in her litter, and all of them had at least one black paw.

"Is that a Siamese cat?" Jaime asked, pointing at one.

"I think so, or at least part Siamese," I said.

"Aren't those really expensive?" she asked.

"I think so, but I guess things happen, cats get lost. There is also a calico cat, a lot of mixes, a Himalayan—"

"That's a part of India, in the mountains!" Rupinder said. "Which one is that?"

"It's the one with the long gray fur. It must get cold in the mountains," I said.

"He is certainly the most beautiful cat," Rupinder said.

"I know that type of cat," Mohammad said, pointing out a sleek, thin cat. "It is at least part Abyssinian. They're from Somalia and the Middle East."

"I thought he looked like those cats carved onto the walls of the pyramids," I said. "And if we're going by nationality, then Alexander should pay particular attention to that grayish blue cat right over there. That one is a Russian Blue."

"Very nice cat," Alexander said. He tossed a piece of his lunch at the feet of the Blue. "From one Russian to another. I will give him a Russian name—I will call him Kot."

"What does that mean?" Jaime asked.

"It means cat, because he is a cat," said Alexander.

"Hold on, if Alexander gets to name a cat, we all should get to name one too," Rupinder said.

"Yeah!" Jaime added.

Mohammad and Devon nodded in agreement.

"You can all name two if you want," I said.

They all cheered and the cats startled before settling back in to eat.

"If Alexander names the Russian Blue, then I want to name the Himalayan," Rupinder said.

"And Siam is sort of close to China, so the Siamese should be mine to name," Jaime said.

"Sure, of course," I said.

"And Mohammad gets that other cat, but where does that leave me?" Devon asked. "Are there any special types of cats from Jamaica?"

"I'm not sure, but how about we find out the way I found out about all the other cats," I said.

"How *did* you get to know so much about cats?" Jaime asked.

"It's like Mr. Spence says, the more you read, the more you know. I've been taking books out of the library. Our teacher-librarian, Miss Hobbs, is super helpful. She really *likes* it when you take out books. She showed me sites on the Internet too. She said reading is reading, whether it's in a book or on the Internet or on the back of a cereal box."

"Then I'm reading every morning at breakfast," Simon said. "Do you think Mr. Spence would let me do a reading journal entry on Cheerios?"

"Give it a try," I said.

King leaped forward and chased away a couple of the smaller cats, grabbing their food.

"That big cat is such a bully," Devon said. "If Mr. Spence was here, he'd have a talk with him."

"I call that cat King, because he runs the place."

"He's still a big bully," Devon said, "and I don't like him."

"Me neither," I admitted.

"Is your favorite cat here?" Simon asked me.

"No, I don't see Hunter. I call him that because he's the best hunter," I explained to the others. "When I do see him, he often has something that he's caught. Even if he was here, he probably wouldn't take our food. He's too proud."

"Probably too well fed," Simon said.

"He *is* a very good hunter," I said.

We leaned against an old car and watched the cats finish their meal.

"Can we do this again another time?" Rupinder asked.

"Yeah, can we?" Mohammad asked.

I turned to Mr. Singh, as did everybody else.

"If you are friends of Taylor and Simon, then you are good kids and most welcome," Mr. Singh said.

A cheer rose up and a few cats ran away. King glared

at us angrily for disturbing his meal. And then I saw Hunter.

He was sitting off to the side, partially hidden in the shadows. He was watching us. He was watching everything. Our eyes locked. He saw me, and I saw him. His eyes were soft. He wasn't glaring at me.

Twelve

I exited through the hole in the fence quickly. I'd lost track of time, but I knew it was getting late, so I didn't even stop to say goodbye to Mr. Singh at the front gate. Simon was in after-school math classes. I was by myself, and I didn't want to be in the junkyard alone after dark.

I also wanted to get home before my mother arrived. Even though she was working longer hours, I often didn't get home much earlier than she did. If I wasn't there when she arrived, she would worry. She was starting to become concerned about how much time I was spending with the cats. She hadn't exactly told me that, but her comments and expressions gave away what she was really feeling.

The other thing that made me want to hurry was the setting sun. I was still nervous being out alone at night. Not that it was ever completely dark in the city.

The fastest way home was through the back alleys. There was no way I'd go that way after dark, especially alone, but it wasn't dark yet. If I moved fast enough, I'd be home before it got *officially* dark. That made the decision for me. I cut into the alley.

On one side were the back fences of houses. On the other side were the backs of stores and restaurants. I walked down the center of the alley.

I could hear voices coming from both sides, radios and tvs playing, and the sound of machinery operating in small shops. The bakery was really noisy. The Italian Bakery had its doors open, and I could see rows and rows of trays holding goodies. There was a strong smell of curry from the Indian restaurant. The aroma of the French fries from a fast-food restaurant was coming out through the exhaust fan. My mouth almost started to water.

But all of the wonderful smells mixed with the pungent odor of the garbage bins, which weren't as mouthwatering. Some of the bins were open, but most of them were sealed up. As I walked, I alternated between my mouth watering and my stomach feeling like it might want to heave.

Out of the corner of my eye, I saw a dark shape moving in the shadows at the side of a building. It was large—some sort of animal. It leaped up onto a garbage can. It was Hunter! His back was to me, and the noise from the store's big exhaust fan blocked out any chance he'd hear me.

I stopped and backed into the bushes and weeds on the far side of the alley. I wanted to see what he was up to. Maybe I would even see his hunting skills in action.

It was cool to be the one doing the observing for a change. I wondered how long it would take for him to notice me.

I knew cats have better eyesight than people, but they don't see details as much as they see movement. If I didn't move, there was a good chance I would be invisible to Hunter. My new superpowers were coming in handy after all!

Hunter walked along a row of sealed garbage cans. Was he looking for a rodent or a missing lid? He spun around, and his eyes glowed like two little green laser beams straight at me. I thought he heard me, but his head kept turning to the left, and a dog came out of the shadows. No, not a dog—its movements were different, more waddling than walking. It was a raccoon! All I could see was its big backside as it moved toward Hunter.

Hunter leaped up onto a ledge above the garbage cans. There was no way the big fat raccoon could get up there. Hunter sat on his perch. His tail swished back and forth, and his eyes burned. He didn't look happy.

The raccoon approached the garbage can where Hunter had been. It stretched up, standing on its back legs. It was gigantic, as tall as the can and nearly as wide!

It pushed against the can, gripping the top with its hands and wobbling the can back and forth until it finally tumbled over, hitting the pavement with a tremendous crash.

I'd thought the lid would pop open, but it didn't. The raccoon fumbled with the lid, and the can rocked and rolled back and forth on the pavement. It looked like it was sealed too tightly for the raccoon's small hands to open, but then it popped off. A pile of garbage poured onto the pavement. The raccoon sat on its haunches and began to pick through the garbage.

Hunter stood up. He walked along the ledge, looking down at the raccoon. Was he going to pounce on it? It wasn't a mouse or a rat. It was an animal almost as large as a small bear.

I tried to remember what I knew about raccoons. They were clever and had hands like monkeys. They liked to wash their food before they ate it. But unless there was a bottle of water in the garbage can, that wasn't going to happen. What I couldn't remember was if they ate plants or meat or both. And if they ate meat, was *cat* part of their regular diet?

Hunter jumped down from the ledge onto one of the cans. If he'd made any sound, I couldn't hear it over the exhaust fan. Could the raccoon hear him? It seemed too busy with its dinner to notice anything.

Hunter moved stealthily, low, ears back, tail flat. He was stalking the raccoon. He was going to attack it, even though the raccoon was three times as big as him!

The raccoon looked up, and the two animals locked eyes. The raccoon opened its mouth and let out a cry. For a second I saw a set of shiny, sharp teeth.

Hunter jumped to the ground and crept forward until the two animals were no more than a few feet apart. He crouched down and looked like he was about to pounce. They were now so close, Hunter was partially hidden from my view by the bulk of the raccoon. This was crazy. He could be hurt or even killed!

The raccoon leaned into the garbage can, pulled something out and tossed it to Hunter. Hunter smelled it, sat down and started to eat. I was stunned. What had just happened?

The raccoon began eating again. The two of them weren't going to fight. They were having *dinner* together!

I chuckled and the two of them turned in my direction. I felt as if I'd been caught doing something wrong. I expected them to run away, but they just sat there, staring. They looked at each other, then at me, and then back at each other. I got the feeling they were having a conversation about what to do about me. I wouldn't have been surprised if the raccoon reached into the garbage and threw a tidbit my way.

"It's okay," I said. "I'm just going to leave now."

The raccoon tilted its head to one side as if it understood what I was saying but was trying to figure out why I would leave. Then the two of them turned back to their meal.

I wanted to watch, but it was getting late. I took off, hoping to get home before both the darkness and my mother.

Thirteen

"I feel like I'm doing something I shouldn't," my mother said.

"It does have that feeling," I agreed as I pulled the chain-link fence back to widen the hole.

"I thought you usually went in through the front gate."

"I do when Mr. Singh is working," I said.

"So he's not working today?"

"It's Sunday. No weekends, no evenings."

My mother stepped through and chuckled.

"What's so funny?"

"I was just thinking of the headlines. 'Newly promoted assistant bank manager and son arrested for break and entry at junkyard. Film at eleven.'"

"Just remember the camera adds ten pounds," I said.

"Great, I'll be a felon who looks like she needs to go on a diet."

We walked through the yard.

"I've never been in a junkyard before," she said. Her head swiveled from side to side. "It's a bit spooky."

"It's not spooky. Well, not *that* spooky."

"It's just the sort of place you'd see on one of those *CSI* episodes where they find a body or there's a killer or—"

"I used to think the same thing."

"But not now?" she asked.

"Not until you brought it up. You're creeping me out."

"Sorry," she said.

Of course it didn't feel creepy to me anymore. The junkyard was like a second home, a second home that could be a scene from *CSI Toronto*.

"I'm just a little nervous. I really do want to see the cats, and I guess there's no other way," she said.

"It's not like I can bring them around to the apartment."

"You talk so much about them, I think I'll even be able to pick them out, especially the ones like Miss Mittens and King and Hunter."

"Hunter is the least likely to be here," I said.

"That's strange. You talk about him the most."

"I do?"

"Definitely. I get the feeling he's your favorite."

"I guess he is," I said.

"Oh my goodness!" My mother shrieked and skidded to a stop.

Right in front of us, directly in our path, was a raccoon. It was the same raccoon I'd first seen with Hunter in the alley. I had seen it in the junkyard a couple of times since then. He heard us, stopped, spun around and sat down, staring at us.

"Don't worry, it's just Rocky," I said.

"Rocky?"

"I named him," I said. "You know that song you listen to by that group, what is it called, the Beatles?"

"Oh, 'Rocky Raccoon'!" she said and sang a couple of bars from the song. "I can't believe how big it is."

"He is big, but he never bothers me. I think he lives around here too," I said. "But from what Mr. Singh has told me, he doesn't live in the yard."

"Raccoons can be dangerous," she said. "Especially one that big. They have very sharp claws and can be vicious. I read somewhere they get rabies and—"

"Rocky doesn't have rabies," I said. "And he isn't vicious. He's pretty relaxed."

It looked like Rocky had a smile on his face, like he had a secret or had just been told a joke.

"Actually," my mother said and chuckled, "his expression—this is going to sound strange—it looks a bit like Mona Lisa's smile. Well, if she was furry and wearing a black mask."

"I can see that," I said, "but he reminds me of somebody else. With that big belly, the way he's sitting and that thoughtful look, I was thinking that he looked like a furry Buddha."

"I can see that too!" she exclaimed. "He does look wise, like he's sitting there contemplating life."

"Thinking that wouldn't offend anybody, would it?" I asked. "You know, comparing a raccoon to Buddha. That wouldn't make people who believe in Buddha mad, would it?"

"I think Buddhists are a pretty understanding people," she said. "Besides, they believe in reincarnation. For all we know, coming back as a raccoon may be a higher life form than a person."

I laughed.

"Either way, he's such a chubby guy, he seems to be doing fairly well for himself," she said. "Maybe he just got a promotion too."

Rocky tilted his head to the side as if he was trying to figure us out. He shook a paw at us, like he was waving goodbye, turned around and slowly waddled away.

"Any more surprise animals I should know about?" she asked.

"There is a family of skunks, a mother and a couple of kittens," I said. "But I don't think we'll see them this early in the morning. They sleep during the day, so I've only seen them in the evenings. Mr. Singh thinks they live under an abandoned warehouse in the alley."

"Good to know."

I almost mentioned the rats but thought better of it. We weren't going near where most of them lived.

"It's not much farther. It's just around this—"

There were three people standing there—a man and two women, one young and one older. They were tossing food to the cats. I'd never seen anybody else here except the mean bully boys from before. It was a little unnerving, but it was good to know my friends and I weren't the only ones who cared about the cats.

Then I noticed the traps.

Fourteen

"Leave those cats alone!" I screamed and ran toward them.

"Taylor!" my mother yelled.

The three people looked shocked, stunned, as I raced forward.

"Get away from those cats, *now!*" I ordered them.

They stumbled backward, staring at me like I was insane. "It's all right," the man said.

"It's not all right!" I yelled back. I ran past them toward the cats. "Shoo! Get away!"

Most of the cats scattered, dropping bits of food and disappearing into the cars. A couple of the cats hissed at me, and King just stood there, standing his ground, glaring. His fur bristled and made him look even bigger. He wasn't giving up his food.

I bent down, grabbed a rock and skipped it toward him, trying not to hit him. He ran off, giving me a threatening glare before he too disappeared.

"You shouldn't throw rocks at the cats!" the man exclaimed.

"Maybe you shouldn't be throwing poisoned meat at them!" I yelled back.

"Poisoned meat?" he said. "What are you—?"

"Get out of here, now!" I ordered. I picked up two more rocks. "Or else!"

My mother rushed forward. "How about if everybody calms down!" she said. She didn't sound very calm.

"Yes, let's be reasonable," the man said.

"Reasonable people don't poison innocent cats!" I said.

"We weren't poisoning them!" he said.

"Honestly, we were helping them!" the older woman said.

"Helping them into those cages? You all should be ashamed of yourselves!" I called out.

"Son, we weren't doing anything wrong," he said.

"I'm not your son. I'm going to get the security guard and get him to call the police and have you all arrested!"

"Please don't call anybody," the man pleaded.

"If you're not doing anything wrong, then why don't you want me to call the police?" I asked.

My mother nodded in agreement.

The man let out a sigh. "We're not harming the cats, but we also don't have permission to be here. Technically, we're trespassing."

"Well, we *do* have permission to be here," I said.

"We came in through a hole in the fence," the younger woman said. She sounded guilty.

"Then since you know how to come in through the hole, you know how to go *out* through the hole before I call the police. Understand?" I asked.

"Look, let me explain. My name is Curtis. Curtis Reynolds. *Doctor* Reynolds. I'm a veterinarian," the man said.

"You're a vet?" I asked.

"I am."

"How do we know you really are a vet?" my mother asked. That was a good question. "I could say I was the Queen of Toronto, but that doesn't make it true."

"Here, I have some business cards." He dug into his pocket and pulled out the cards, handing one to me and the other to my mother. In raised letters it said: *Dr. Reynolds, DVM, Small Animals and Emergency Medicine.* He *was* a vet.

"So you have a card. That only means you have a computer and a printer," my mother said.

Another good point I hadn't thought of. "Even if you are a vet, that doesn't explain what you're doing here," I said.

"What we're doing is trying to help," Dr. Reynolds said. "This is Doris." He gestured to the older woman. "And this is Sarah. We were trying to help the cats."

"And how do those traps help the cats?" I asked.

"If a cat is badly injured or needs medical treatment, we trap it so Dr. Reynolds can treat it," Doris said. "When they're well enough, we bring them back."

"The food you were giving them wasn't poisoned?" I asked.

"Of course not!" Sarah said. "What sort of evil person would do that to a living creature?"

"There is something in the food," Dr. Reynolds said. "We put antibiotics and medications into the food to inoculate the cats."

"So you really are trying to help them," I said.

"We're members of the Feral Cat Association of Toronto," Dr. Reynolds explained.

"Or F-Cat for short," Sarah said.

"It's a group of people who work together to try to help wild cats, feral cats," Doris said.

"There are a few dozen of us," Sarah added. "Some people make donations, others donate time to help feed them."

"Or treat them," Doris said. "Like Dr. Reynolds."

It all sounded good, but I was still suspicious. "I've never seen anybody here before," I said.

"We've never been here before. We just found out about this colony a few weeks ago. This is the first time we could get here. There are hundreds of feral cat colonies in the city."

"That's hard to believe," my mother said.

"Most people find it hard to believe," Doris said. "Before I got involved, I had no idea there could possibly be so many."

"But where are they all?" I asked. "It's not like there are hundreds of junkyards."

"Often they live in industrial sites like this, but also in abandoned houses and under bridges," Sarah said.

"We also find them in fields, ravines and public spaces like parks," Dr. Reynolds added. "Both the Scarborough Bluffs and the Leslie Street Spit are home to two very large colonies. Cats are perfect animals to create feral colonies."

"Yes," Doris said, "they multiply quickly and they're very social. So they like to live in groups."

"Plus, they are mobile, independent by nature, can catch or scrounge for food and, really, are only semi-domesticated even when they live with people," Dr. Reynolds said.

"Nobody really owns a cat," I said. Since Mr. Singh had first said that, I'd come to believe it.

"I'm glad you think that way," Dr. Reynolds said. "So many people think that feral cats are lost house cats that only need a little affection and a scratch behind their ears."

"With some of them, it would be a great way to lose a finger," I said.

"But not all of them," Doris said. "Some are just a few months away from being house cats and can be very gentle."

"And others are very savage," Dr. Reynolds said. "How many cats do you think are in this colony?"

"I know of forty-three cats and some kittens," I said.

"Are you sure of those numbers?" Dr. Reynolds asked. "It's difficult to distinguish individuals and get an accurate count of the residents."

"I'm completely sure," I said. "I know them, cat by cat."

"My son spends a lot of time here," my mother said. "He really cares for these cats."

"We thought somebody had taken an interest in them," Doris said. "These cats are in excellent shape."

"You'll notice the traps are empty," Dr. Reynolds said. "These cats are healthy. Thick fur, well fed, perhaps a little bit too well fed. That one tabby is *enormous!*"

"That's King," I said.

"You've named them?" Dr. Reynolds asked.

"Not all of them. Just the most important ones," I said.

"And he's called King because he's the dominant tomcat, right?" Dr. Reynolds asked.

"Him and another cat," I said.

"There's another cat as big as him?" Dr. Reynolds questioned.

"He's not that big. He's sort of long and athletic," I said. "Does that sound strange, to call a cat athletic?"

"Not strange at all. All cats are athletes," Dr. Reynolds said.

"But this one is even more than the others. He can really jump, and he's a great hunter. He's always catching things," I said.

"Does he ever fight King for dominance?" Dr. Reynolds asked.

"I've never seen Hunter and King fight. They know the other is there, but Hunter stays out of King's way."

"That's probably smart. King didn't look like he was going to back down from you," he said.

"I know. That's why I had to toss the rock. I wasn't trying to hit him, just scare him away."

"You never get too close to him, do you?" my mother asked.

"Not close enough to scratch him behind the ears," I said.

"It's not *you* scratching *him* that I'm afraid of," she said.

"Well, if he does, he's received most of his inoculations today from the pills we put in the food he gobbled down."

"That's reassuring," my mother said, although her words and tone of voice didn't match.

As we were talking, some of the cats had returned, tempted by the food still on the ground.

"Let's move a little farther away," I said.

"We should get going," Dr. Reynolds said. "These cats are fine, and we should leave before the security guard finds us."

"It's okay if he does. As long as I tell him you're okay, then you'll be fine."

"That's nice to hear. Most of the property owners don't like us. They see us as encouraging something they don't want to have in the first place," Dr. Reynolds said.

"As long as you tell Mr. Singh you're a friend of Taylor—that's me—then you'll be welcome here."

"That's great. Most owners don't think of feral cats as any better than an infestation of rats," Dr. Reynolds said.

"Mr. Singh isn't the owner. He's the head security guard."

"Well, it's good to have somebody on our side," Dr. Reynolds said. "But we should be going anyway. We want to get to another colony today." He looked around. "Now if we can just find our way out."

"I can show you. If you point me in the direction you came from, I'll know which hole you came through," I said.

All three of them pointed in different directions.

"I guess we got a little turned around," Dr. Reynolds said.

"No problem. I'll show you all the holes in the fence until we find the one you came through."

"Thanks, we appreciate your help, and the help you're giving these cats," Dr. Reynolds said.

He held out his hand. I slipped his business card into my pocket and shook his hand. It was good to know I wasn't alone.

Fifteen

I sat as still as possible, not moving my eyes and trying to control my breathing so my chest didn't go up or down. I'd found the longer I sat still, the more comfortable the cats became with me. It was as if they'd forgotten I was there. I became another hunk of junk in the yard. Or, I liked to imagine, one of them. I even started having cat-like thoughts as I sat motionless.

Over the weeks the cats had let me get closer and closer. Now some of them even let me get close enough to give them a scratch behind the ears. That Doris woman had been right about some of the cats being gentle. I'd learned which ones I could risk doing that with. Not that I was going to tell my mother.

The best way to get close to them was to wait and be patient. I always let them approach me. I never approached them. It was mainly the teenager cats and the kittens, but a couple of the older cats, including Miss Mittens, allowed me to stroke them on the back too. Some of them even brushed against my leg or stood on their hind legs to meet my hand halfway.

I wasn't sure what Dr. Reynolds would have thought, but I knew my mother would not approve. Mr. Singh had seen me patting the cats, as had Simon, and the other guys and Jaime. They were a little jealous because the cats wouldn't let any of them get close, not even the cats they'd named.

Alexander, of course, called his cat Kot. Jaime named the Burmese and the Siamese cats Minx and Ming. The Himalayan cat was named Sherpa by Rupinder, in honor of the guides who take climbers up Mount Everest, the highest mountain in the world. Mohammad named a calico cat Pizza, because that was his favorite food, and the Abyssinian Cleopatra, because she reminded him of a carving on a pyramid. And finally, Devon named an orange tabby Marley, after Bob Marley.

They may have named some of the cats, but I invested the most time and energy at the colony. Simon spent more time there than anybody else except me, but he had trouble sitting still or staying quiet long enough to allow the cats to approach. He was a great guy, but patience wasn't one of his virtues.

Sitting off to the side was King. He was keeping an eye on me but pretending not to. I didn't think he was worried about me as much as he wanted to know if I had any food. His interest in me was strictly related to the food I brought. He didn't seem to want or need human contact. In fact, he didn't even seem interested in the other cats.

After Dr. Reynolds had questioned the relationship between King and Hunter, I'd noticed that King never fought with Hunter. Of course Hunter wasn't nearly as big, but he had a way about him that left little doubt he could handle himself. King was a bully, and bullies didn't usually pick on somebody who could actually fight back. Not that Hunter would win a fight with King. King was big and seemed to be getting bigger due to all the extra food I'd been bringing to the colony. So Hunter gave King his space and King gave Hunter his space.

I heard the sound of pounding feet, lots of them, loud and fast. I spun around in time to see two dogs run into the clearing. One was big and the other bigger. The big one looked like some sort of Rottweiler and German shepherd cross. The other just looked mean. One of its ears was up and the other looked as if it had been torn off. The two of them almost merged into one gigantic, eight-legged mass of black, brown and white fur. They raced into the clearing, slowing slightly and then racing straight toward us. Before I could react, or even think to react, they charged the cats. There was a scramble as cats and kittens scattered into the shelter of the wrecks. The dogs raced through, turning and twisting, trying to catch all the cats but not being able to focus on any of them.

One of the dogs grabbed a kitten, throwing it up into the air. The kitten hit the ground, rolling and tumbling, and the dogs chased after it as it raced away for its life.

A black blur came shooting out of nowhere. It was Hunter, and he landed on the back of the larger dog. The dog howled as Hunter dug in his claws, hanging on to the dog, riding him like a horse. The dog jumped and leaped and roared, desperate to shake Hunter loose. He reached back, tried to grab Hunter with his teeth, but the cat struck him in the face and the dog howled again. The dog tripped and rolled over, and Hunter leaped off, landing against one of the wrecked cars.

Before Hunter could scramble to his feet, the second dog came forward and charged toward him. Hunter crouched, puffed out his fur, hissed and snarled. The dog stopped in his tracks. The first dog, blood dripping down its side, flanked the second. Together the dogs growled and inched forward. Why wasn't Hunter running away? Why wasn't he trying to escape? He couldn't fight both of them.

Behind Hunter was a solid mass of metal. There was no place for him to retreat to. He was trapped. They were going to kill him, if they could.

The whole incident unfolded as if it was in slow motion. I was too shocked to move, but I had to do something.

"Hey, go away!" I screamed and stumbled to my feet.

Both dogs turned to look at me. If I could distract them for a few seconds, maybe Hunter could get away.

I reached down and picked up a rock. Without hesitation I whipped it at the dogs. It hit the ground, short and wide. The smaller of the two dogs startled and turned away from Hunter toward me. It growled, and the big dog started barking.

The dogs' eyes glowered. Their teeth were bared, and they growled ominously. Suddenly it wasn't only Hunter I was scared for. I looked around. There had to be some place for me to go if they charged.

If I climbed on top of a wreck or inside one of the cars, they wouldn't be able to get me. I could probably get away before they could reach me, but I wasn't going to abandon Hunter.

I quickly looked around for something I could use to defend myself. On the ground was a hubcap, and beside it was a long metal pipe. I grabbed both, holding one in front of me like a shield and the other like a sword. I was like a knight, but a knight without armor, or a horse. Worse, I was a knight who was scared to death. So much for being Catboy. Where was that potato peeler when I needed it?

I slammed the pipe against the ground with a thud. The dogs spun around, more interested in me than in Hunter.

"Get away, Hunter!" I screamed. "Run, you stupid cat!"

He didn't run. He stood his ground, and I got the feeling he didn't want to abandon me. If he ran, the dogs would focus all their attention on me. Who was saving who here?

I slammed the pole against the ground again. The dogs turned away from Hunter and shied away, ever so slightly, from me. They started backing up. They were more afraid of me than I was of them. Hunter wasn't going anywhere.

I took another step forward and the dogs retreated a little more. Unfortunately they were retreating toward Hunter. There was only one thing to do.

I took a deep breath and charged at the dogs, swinging the pole, clanging it against the hubcap and screaming at the top of my lungs! The dogs jumped, one yelped, and they both ran off with their tails between their legs.

I skidded to a stop and dropped the pole and hubcap. They were gone. I bent over, exhausted, and tried to get my breath back. I realized I was shaking. I looked up at Hunter. He was still there. He hadn't run. He lowered his head slightly, as if he was nodding at me, acknowledging what I'd done. Then he turned, limped away, his front right paw barely touching the ground, and disappeared into the wrecks.

Sixteen

"I can hardly see in there," Dr. Reynolds said. "Are you sure that's even him?"

"It's him," I said. "That's where he's been for the last three days."

The day after the dog fight, I hadn't been able to find Hunter. I'd convinced myself he was okay and must be out hunting, exploring, roaming the streets. But the next day I found him sitting outside a narrow cranny where he was holed up. Unable to catch anything, he'd become hungry enough to accept my charity.

I'd hoped if I fed him for a few days, his leg would heal. Instead, it was getting worse. It was so swollen he wouldn't let it touch the ground at all now, and he hobbled around on three legs.

The third day I decided to get help. I'd kept Dr. Reynolds's card. When I called his number, I expected to get a secretary or receptionist and be given excuses as to why he wasn't available or be told he'd call me back, or maybe I'd hear from him in a few days or a week. Instead, he answered the phone on the first ring, and here we were, less than an hour later, in the junkyard.

"I can't assess him if I can't see him," Dr. Reynolds said.

"I can probably get him to come out," I said. I dug into my pocket and pulled out a piece of baloney. "I'll toss this and—"

"No, wait," Dr. Reynolds said. "He's probably hungry and food is the only thing we have going for us. Pass me that."

I handed him the baloney, and he placed it inside the trap he'd brought.

"What if you put antibiotics in the meat? Would that help?" I asked.

"It might, but it's risky. It might not be all he needs, and if we feed him we lose the only advantage we have— his hunger. With the baloney, I'm hoping to lure him into the trap." He paused. "I know you don't want to trap him. It doesn't feel right, does it?"

I shook my head. It felt like we were tricking him.

Dr. Reynolds put the trap down beside Hunter's hiding spot. "Now we have to move away, so he'll take the bait."

It *didn't* feel right, but I had to trust the vet. What other choice was there? We shuffled back to the edge of the clearing and hoped Hunter would enter the cage and trip the door shut.

"So we just wait?" I asked.

"Wait and hope none of the other cats get in the trap instead."

"I think we've scared the other cats away," I said.

"They haven't gone far, and that baloney will draw them out of wherever they've—there he is," Dr. Reynolds said, under his breath.

Hunter peeked out of the cranny. He looked around. He could smell the baloney, but he wasn't sure where it was. His injured paw was too swollen and infected to bear any weight.

He crept toward the trap. He smelled the meat, but he was nervous about the trap.

He took a few tentative steps into the opening of the trap.

"Just a little bit farther," Dr. Reynolds whispered. "Get in there."

Hunter hesitated with his head inside and his body outside the trap. He knew something wasn't right and backed out. I knew if he could feed himself he would never have entered the trap.

He peered into the trap, trying to reach the meat without committing to going in. He couldn't do it. He limped forward and was almost all the way inside.

"Come on," Dr. Reynolds said.

Hunter edged forward and the door slammed shut. Hunter jumped, spun around and clawed at the closed door.

"We got him!" Dr. Reynolds said and jumped to his feet.

I trailed behind him as he ran to the trap. Hunter bashed against the sides of the trap, trying desperately to escape.

"It's okay," Dr. Reynolds said. "You're going to be fine."

Hunter hissed and snarled.

"He's not very happy about this," Dr. Reynolds said, stating the obvious.

"I'm not too happy either," I said.

"I know it feels cruel, but what choice did we have?" he asked.

"I know."

Hunter's eyes were bright and angry but he wasn't looking at Dr. Reynolds. He was staring straight at me.

I pretended to look at the magazine. My mother sat next to me and pretended to look at another magazine. All Dr. Reynolds had to read was either really old or titled *Vet's World*—a magazine written for vets, not people sitting in a vet's waiting room. I was so glad we had great books to read in my classroom and the school library. Nobody would read to succeed if these magazines were all the students had to choose from.

According to the clock on the wall, it was just after seven in the evening. We'd been waiting for over two hours. The vet's office had closed at five, and we'd arrived in time to see the last of the other patients and the receptionist leave for the weekend.

I heard the door open and looked up. It was Dr. Reynolds.

I jumped to my feet. "How is he?"

Dr. Reynolds smiled, and I knew the answer. "He's going to be fine," the vet said.

"Can we see him?" I asked.

"Of course, but he won't be able to see you for a while. He's still knocked out from the medication I gave him for the surgery."

Dr. Reynolds explained to us that the infection had been so bad, surgery was the only way to fix Hunter's foot.

He led us into the back. The walls were lined with large and small cages. Some were empty but others held dogs and a few cats. We were greeted by barking, meowing, whining and whimpering. Some of the animals pushed against the bars, trying to get our attention. Others hid at the back of their cage.

"Here he is," Dr. Reynolds said and stopped in front of a small cage.

Hunter was at the back of the cage, unconscious. Dr. Reynolds opened the cage and reached in. "The leg was badly infected. I had to open it up and drain the infection."

"What would have happened if you hadn't done that?" I asked.

"He would have died. But now he'll be fine. He just needs to be given antibiotics for the next few days and watched to make sure the infection improves."

"That's great. Then he can be released, right?"

"Released, as good as new," Dr. Reynolds said.

"And I can be there, right?" I asked.

"Of course you'll be there."

"And can I come here and see him before he's released?"

Dr. Reynolds looked confused. "I'm sorry. I guess I didn't explain. He can't stay here."

"He can't?" my mother asked.

"I don't own this practice. The doctor who does lets me use his operating and examination rooms when they're not being used, after hours and on weekends, but I can't keep animals here."

"But where will he stay?" I asked.

"I assumed you two could keep him."

I looked at my mother. Dr. Reynolds looked at her.

"Do I really have a choice?" she asked.

I threw my arms around her. "Thanks, Mom, thanks so much!"

Seventeen

Hunter stared at me through the bars of the cage, which was better than glaring. We had set him on the floor of our living room.

His cage was big. It had a place to sleep in one corner and a litter box in the other. There was also a slot where I could slip food and water in without having to open the door. If he got loose, I'd never get him back inside and somebody—him, me or both of us—would get hurt.

"I'm glad you've finally decided to stop hissing at me," I said.

I kept up a running commentary around him. It seemed to have a calming effect on both of us.

Although, the first day, nothing short of a tranquilizer would have calmed him. He hissed and snarled and glared nonstop. If looks could kill, I would have been dead a thousand times over.

Day two had been better. The glares continued, but the hissing finally stopped. Thank goodness. It had really started to get to me. And when he stopped hissing, he started eating. The hunger strike had been a problem. Not because he wasn't getting the food he needed to recover, but because he wasn't getting the medication embedded in the food that was essential to his healing. Dr. Reynolds had told me the greatest danger was post-operative infection, and scraping around in a litter box with a newly stitched foot was a recipe for renewed infection.

I gave Hunter the medication the way Dr. Reynolds had shown me. I ground up the pill until it was a fine powder and sprinkled it inside a piece of chicken. Hunter was, as I had always suspected, partial to chicken.

In the junkyard, he'd always been hesitant to take the food I threw him. I knew he was nervous about taking food from people, but I liked to think he wanted to leave it for the kittens or he was too proud to take handouts.

Of course, none of those were issues for King. He would eat anything thrown his way and swat at any cat that got in his way.

It was reassuring to see Hunter's foot getting better. There was no swelling anymore—or at least none I could see. He was putting weight on it too. In fact, he was doing so well he'd even taken a swipe at me when I got too close.

"I don't blame you for having an attitude," I said to him.

I really couldn't blame him for anything—not the hissing, glaring, distrust or wanting to take a shot at me. He'd woken up in a cage in our apartment and was probably still in pain. I didn't want him to be angry with me any more than I wanted him to be afraid. Over the past few months, I thought we'd developed an agreement. Not a friendship, but at least an understanding that I wasn't trying to harm him, and I was a *good* human.

"I'm going to come a little bit closer now."

I moved toward the cage. His eyes burned with intensity and then faded to a soft glow. He wanted to see what I had. He associated me with food as well as imprisonment. I was sure he smelled the chicken in the container I carried.

"You're looking good today. How's the foot feeling?"

He didn't answer, although he looked like he was giving my question some thought.

I bent down so I was at eye-level with him. He stayed in the center of the cage instead of retreating into the far corner. Maybe he'd finally come to realize I wasn't going to hurt him, I was going to feed him.

I held a piece of chicken out. His ears perked up and he let out a soft, plaintive cry, as if he was asking if the food was for him.

"Of course it's yours," I said. "Do you see any other cats around here?"

Instantly, I felt bad. Of course there were no other cats. Hunter was by himself because I'd taken him away from his family, his colony.

"You'll be back soon. I bet they really miss you."

The other cats were probably missing him and wondering where he went. Did they feel abandoned? Were they worried or were they grieving? Had they sent out a cat search party to look for him? And what about the cats who depended on him for food? Were there kittens going to sleep hungry because Hunter hadn't brought anything for them?

I knew King was "the king" of the colony, but I thought Hunter was the glue that held it together. Without him, things wouldn't be the same.

Hunter let out another little cry, louder this time, as if he was chiding me for forgetting who the chicken in my hands was for.

"Sorry," I said. "I got distracted. Thinking."

I leaned closer to the bars, and Hunter did the same on his side. I carefully extended my hand, putting the piece of meat up to the bars. Hunter put his mouth up against the cage and gently took the chicken from my fingers. I smiled.

Unbelievable. In three days he had gone from wanting to scratch out my eyes to eating from my fingers.

If he'd come this far in three days what would happen if I kept him with me for a week or two? Could he become more than a cat in a cage? Could he...?

I stopped myself. Of course he couldn't. I knew that. It's just that the apartment wasn't as lonely when he was here.

I lay on my belly with my face pressed against the bars. I pulled out another piece of chicken. This one was filled with the medicine. I always made a point of giving him one "good" piece first, before giving him the piece that might taste bad because of the medicine.

He gently took that second piece from my fingers. I felt his teeth brush against my fingertips. A bite— even an accidental one—wouldn't have been good. It would have been hard to explain to my mother. But at least she'd know it wasn't a health problem. Hunter was fully inoculated from his shots after the surgery.

Besides, Dr. Reynolds had explained a cat bite wasn't nearly as bad for germs as a human bite, not that any humans had bitten me recently!

I was grateful when Hunter gobbled down the medicated chicken. I tossed another piece through the bars and he grabbed it midair and swallowed it without chewing.

I took the rest of the pieces and slid them through the slot leading to the food dish. I was deliberately overfeeding him so he'd have a little extra weight when he was released, just in case he wasn't able to hunt as effectively for a while.

"Enjoy your meal, Hunter. It's your last before you go home."

He stopped eating and looked up at me. If I didn't know better, I would have sworn he understood.

"You're going home today. Well, maybe."

Dr. Reynolds was coming over to do an exam, and if it went well, Hunter would be set free.

"I know this has been hard. But we had to do it. We had no choice."

I hoped he understood and could forgive me. I'd only been to the colony briefly in the last few days. Simon, Jaime and the guys, with help from Mr. Singh, had been taking care of feeding them.

Wait, what was that sound? It was like a small motor or…Hunter was purring. He was rubbing his face against the bars and purring!

I slowly moved my hand closer. I put it flat against the bars. He didn't pull away. Instead, he pressed harder, and I felt fur against my hand. This wasn't an accident. He knew my hand was there. He knew I was petting him. His little engine got louder. I was so happy I thought I might start purring myself!

Eighteen

"I'd offer to help, but I think it's better if it's just you,"
Dr. Reynolds said.

"I think you're right."

I pulled the cage out of the back of his vehicle. It was
heavy and awkward.

"I could help," my mother offered.

"No, Dr. Reynolds is right. Hunter is more comfortable with just me."

"No argument there," she said.

Hunter crouched down in the cage, trying to main-
tain his balance as I walked away with him. If anybody
else approached, he'd start to hiss and snarl. He might
even try to strike at them through the bars. I was

wearing the thick work gloves Dr. Reynolds insisted I wear—that my mother *really* insisted I wear. She was wearing a pair too, even though she wasn't planning to get near Hunter.

She and Hunter had coexisted in our apartment, but they hadn't interacted much. They both kept an eye on each other, but their fears were very different. My mother was afraid he wasn't ever going to leave, that somehow he was going to become "our cat."

She hadn't said it in so many words, I just knew. Really, she had nothing to worry about. Despite my random thoughts about keeping him—thoughts I would *never* say to her—Hunter was a feral cat. He was wild, born and raised. There was no way he could ever become a pet. No way. He tolerated me, but that was a far cry from being a house cat.

Besides, Hunter didn't belong in an apartment. His world was out here. Locking him up in a cage— and really, our apartment was just a big cage—was like putting him in jail. He'd committed no crime and didn't deserve to be imprisoned. Life on the streets was harder and shorter, but it was his life.

And there was one other factor. The other cats. Hunter had lived as part of a large extended family, and in my apartment he was all by himself. It wasn't just prison, it was solitary confinement. Moving to the city, away from everybody I knew, made me more understanding.

Hunter shifted around in the cage. He recognized the junkyard and probably smelled his family.

He let out a loud cry, and I almost lost my grip on the cage.

"He's telling them he's home," I said. "Do you think they missed him?"

"I'm sure they had an awareness of his absence, of him being gone," Dr. Reynolds said. "But 'missed' might be the wrong term."

"I'm sure they missed him. At least some of them must have," I said.

"We have to be careful not to anthropomorphize animals," he said.

"What?"

"*Anthropomorphize.* It means giving animals or inanimate objects human characteristics or qualities."

"I'm not even sure I can pronounce that, so I don't think I'm doing it. Am I?"

"I think you could be. Sometimes we refer to a rock being stubborn or the wind being angry. That is anthropomorphizing. People are stubborn or angry, not rocks or wind," he said.

"But I'm not talking about a rock. I'm talking about an animal with feelings and emotions and—"

"It applies to animals as well," said Dr. Reynolds. "Cats do have feelings and emotions, but they're *cat* feelings and emotions. For example, the concept of jealousy is a human emotion."

"I think cats feel jealousy," I argued. "I think King is jealous of Hunter sometimes."

"I think the two are in competition, but jealousy is a human emotion." Dr. Reynolds paused. "With animals, especially ones we spend time with regularly, we often ascribe human characteristics to them. But cats don't think or feel the same way we do. So their actions and reasons for doing things aren't the same as ours."

"But some of the other cats must have missed him," I said.

"They knew he wasn't there, and they were probably aware they weren't eating as much, but their whole sense of time and interaction is cat-like, not human-like."

"But they're a family."

"You're right there," he agreed. "I'm sure he *is* the father of some of those kittens. But again, they don't have a sense of family the way we do."

I wasn't going to argue, but I was sure he was wrong. Maybe he was a vet, but even vets didn't know everything. I knew Hunter was missed by some of the other cats, the same way I'd miss my mom if she was gone, or the way I miss my old friends and my grandparents. I was looking forward to seeing them at Christmas.

Hunter let out another cry. It wasn't angry or desperate or scared, or even a warning. It was simply a cry to let the cats know he was back. He was home.

I almost told Dr. Reynolds this, but he wouldn't have believed me.

"We're coming up to the clearing," Dr. Reynolds said. "It's better if we let Taylor go on alone. The fewer people the better."

That at least made sense. Besides, I wanted to have a few seconds alone with Hunter. I had human emotions and feelings, and I was going to miss him.

As soon as I was far enough away that I knew my mother and Dr. Reynolds couldn't hear me, I started to talk to Hunter. "Here we go," I said softly. "You're almost home. I promised you I'd bring you back."

He didn't look up at the sound of my voice. He just stared straight ahead.

"It's like I told you. We only did this to get your leg healed and then I'd bring you back, back to your family."

I entered the clearing and a few cats were already there. A couple of them roused from sleep and another cat got to its feet. It had only been a few days, but they acted like they didn't even remember me.

"They know you're here," I said to Hunter.

I was glad to see the cats, but I wished there were more of them or at least a few of my favorites around. I would have loved to see Miss Mittens. But King not being here was a plus. I didn't like him. He was a mean, selfish…Maybe Dr. Reynolds was right and I was giving them human qualities.

A few other cats poked their heads out of the wrecks, but they were all cautious of my presence.

I put the cage down carefully. All I had to do was open the cage and let Hunter go.

"Well, Hunter," I said. "This is it. I'm going to miss you."

He stared through the bars, ignoring me.

I wanted to say something more, but what was I going to say, and what would he understand even if I said it? He was in the cage and needed to get out. To set him free, I had to open the door, not come up with something "touching" to say. Besides, it wasn't like I wasn't going to see him again.

I fumbled with the latch. My hands were clumsy inside the thick gloves. I pulled off one of the gloves. I flicked the latch and swung the door open, clicking it in place so it wouldn't close on him.

Hunter stayed crouched on his haunches. He didn't move. I'd expected him to bolt as soon as I opened it. But he didn't. The only part of him that moved was the tip of his tail. It twitched back and forth, as if it was a separate being. Slowly he inched forward.

"It's okay to go," I said. "You're free."

He finally looked up through the bars at me. His eyes were bright, but they weren't angry. He moved a few more inches and stopped. He pressed his head against the side of the opening and rubbed his head against it. He was purring. I could hear him purring!

I had to fight the urge to give him a scratch behind his ears.

Before I knew what had happened, Hunter jumped, soared through the opening and landed six feet in front of me. A few of the rock chips scattered, and he scampered forward a dozen more steps and skidded to a stop.

He turned around and faced me. If I didn't know better, I would have sworn he was thinking about what he wanted to say to me, as if *he* was looking for the right words.

"No need for thanks," I said. "Just keeping my word."

He tilted his head to one side.

"And you don't have to say goodbye," I added. "I'll see you tomorrow. Maybe I'll even have some chicken."

His ears perked at the word *chicken*, and I laughed.

"Go on, they're waiting for you," I said.

He turned and walked toward the other cats. He'd gone only a few steps when a flurry of fur surrounded him—it was Miss Mittens's kittens! The four balls of fur practically bowled him off his feet! And right behind them was Miss Mittens. She came up to Hunter and the two of them touched faces—they kissed!

I wanted to call Dr. Reynolds over, but I didn't. I couldn't take my eyes off the cats. I didn't know about any of the other cats in the colony, but these ones were definitely Hunter's family.

He walked toward one of the wrecks, and more cats came out of cracks and crevices. There were at least a dozen, maybe more, in the clearing.

Then King appeared and charged toward Hunter!

King's fur was all puffed out, and he was hissing and snarling. Hunter dodged out of the way. King spun around with lightning speed, swatting a paw at Hunter. Hunter leaped onto the roof of a car. I waited for King to follow him, but he didn't. The two cats glared at each other. Neither moved. Hunter wasn't going to run away, but King wasn't going to jump up on the car either.

Maybe King *couldn't* jump on the car. Hunter, in his cage, had seemed so big. But compared to King, he wasn't. They were about the same height and length, but King was much bigger. And Hunter was still recovering from his injury. He couldn't fight King. Not now.

"Go away, you…you pig!" I yelled. "If you want another meal from me, you'll leave Hunter alone!"

King glared at me. A chill went up my spine. He really would eat me, if he were big enough to do it.

"I guess not everybody is happy to have him back," Dr. Reynolds said as he and my mother appeared at my side.

"Happy? Sounds like somebody is giving the cats human-like qualities," I said.

He laughed. "It does sound like that. I guess it's that he doesn't like having his competition back." Dr. Reynolds paused. "Don't worry. Hunter is smart enough to stay out of his way."

"I hope so."

"So do I. One operation per cat is about all I want to have to do. Let's go so he can settle in."

"Do you want us to leave you alone for a bit?" my mother asked. "You know, to say goodbye?"

"It's not goodbye," I said. "But thanks for offering."

"No problem."

They started off. Hunter and I locked eyes. He nodded his head ever so slightly, as if to say "See you later," and I did the same.

Nineteen

"Excellent work, Taylor!" Mr. Spence said as he handed back my story.

"Thanks." I looked at the mark. It was a level four, an A! "I really enjoyed writing it."

"It shows. And I learned so much about feral cats I didn't know," he said.

"You said, 'Write what you know,' and I know about them."

"You certainly do," he agreed. "But just as impressive was the imagination you put into the story. Writing from the perspective of a cat was a great idea."

"I'm not really a talking-animal sort of guy, but I wanted to try it. Besides, Hunter is more than a cat," I explained.

"He's the leader of the colony, right?"

"He's sort of the *co*-leader of the colony," I said. "Although cats don't really think like that. That would be anthropomo-lo-sizing or something like that."

Mr. Spence smiled. "I think you're aiming for the word *anthropomorphize*."

"Yeah, that's it!"

"That's the wonderful thing about writing. You can give animals, or things, human qualities. Just think, if authors didn't do that we'd have no *Peter Rabbit*, *Charlotte's Web*, *Silverwing*, *Watership Down* or *The Lion, the Witch and the Wardrobe*."

"Not to mention Bugs Bunny or Mickey Mouse," Simon added.

"Or Franklin the Turtle, or the Berenstain Bears," I said. "They were my favorites—you know, when I was a kid."

Mr. Spence laughed. "As opposed to the senior citizen you've become!"

"You know what I mean."

"I do. Besides, you got inside the character of the cat. You saw the world the way a cat who lives in a junkyard, wakes up in a cage in an apartment and is finally being released back into—"

"Excuse me," said a voice over the pa. It was the school secretary.

"Yes," Mr. Spence replied.

"I'm sorry to disturb you," said the secretary. "I have a gentleman in the office who wants to speak to a student in your class. He says it's very important. His name is Mr. Singh."

I smiled when I heard the name Singh.

"Who would he like to speak with?" asked Mr. Spence.

"Taylor," said the secretary.

My stomach did a flip as every eye in the class turned to me. It was *my* Mr. Singh! I had no idea why he would come to school and ask to see me, but it couldn't be good.

Mr. Spence looked at me. "Is he a family member?" he asked.

"He's my friend," I said.

Then the recess bell rang, and Mr. Spence dismissed the class.

"It's okay," Simon said as he passed by. "Whatever it is, it's okay."

I didn't know what to say. Mr. Singh could only be here for one reason—Hunter. He must have taken a turn for the worse, or maybe he'd been hurt by King, or those dogs had come back, or he'd been run over by a car or…There were so many things that could happen to a wild cat. If only I'd kept him in my apartment, he'd be alive and safe and—

"Come, I'll walk you down to the office now," Mr. Spence said.

"Sure, yeah. I'm just a little…a little…"

"Nervous?" said Mr. Spence.

I nodded my head.

"I can understand that, but I am going to come down there with you."

Whatever the problem was, I knew Mr. Spence would help me figure it out. I just hoped I wouldn't cry in front of him if Mr. Singh had bad news for me.

"I don't know why he'd be here to see me," I said. "It has to be important."

We walked into the office, and Mr. Singh stood up and introduced himself to Mr. Spence.

"Taylor, I am most sorry to disturb you at school," Mr. Singh said, "but I wanted to tell you immediately that—"

"Has something happened to Hunter?" I interrupted.

"Hunter is fine," he said. "I saw him this morning. But really, he is not fine. *None* of the cats are fine."

I gasped. "What do you mean?"

"The junkyard…it has been sold."

"Sold?"

"Yes. They are going to turn it into condominiums."

He paused. "And they started this morning."

Twenty

We skidded to a stop outside the fence. "Whoa, some-body stole our hole," Simon said.

Where there should have been a hole in the fence there was none. In fact the whole fence was gone. It had been replaced. Instead of the rusty chain-link fence, a high solid wooden fence had been erected. At regular intervals along the fence, big color posters of the condo-minium tower that was going to be built were displayed. The condo on the poster was tall and sleek with tinted windows and enclosed balconies.

It had been only a week since Mr. Singh first told me what was happening. Already things had changed, and changed quickly. The only thing that hadn't changed was me not coming up with an idea to save the cats. I'd spent time in class and when I couldn't get to sleep at night trying to come up with a plan. It wasn't like a grade-six kid could successfully stop a condo development.

"It's going to be a pretty fancy-looking place," Simon said.

"A pretty expensive-looking place."

"It looks a lot nicer than where we live. I wouldn't mind moving there myself," he said.

I shot him an evil look.

"You know, if it didn't mean taking away the cats' home, no offence," Simon said.

"Sorry," I apologized. "It isn't your fault. If I didn't hate it, I would think it would be a nice place to live too."

"So what do we do now that they've sealed off our entrance?" Simon asked.

"We go to the front entrance."

We circled around the yard. The new fence was solid, and so high we couldn't even see the junk on the other side. The posters listed all the condo's features. It would have an indoor pool, a full exercise facility, underground parking, penthouse terraces, marble and hardwood floors, modern kitchens and concierge services. I didn't know what *concierge* meant, but I didn't like it. It was so slick and beautiful I was sure everybody in the neighborhood would rather have condos here than a junkyard. Well, everybody except me, my friends and the cats.

"Wow, look at that," Simon said.

There were so many images and photos, I didn't know where to look first. "Where?"

"Right here," he said, tapping his hand against the wall where it said *Occupancy*. "People are going to be moving in by next fall."

"Is that even possible?" I asked. "Can they build it that quickly?"

"I guess if there are enough workers, machines and money they can. Besides, it isn't like the owners have to tear anything down before they start building."

He was right. All they had to do was remove the car parts and wrecks. They didn't care about the cats that called the junkyard home. They probably didn't even know about the cats, but telling them wouldn't change anything. To the owners, the cats were even less valuable than the wrecks that littered the lot. At least the scrap metal could be sold for something.

We rounded the corner in time to see a big flatbed truck rumble away from the entrance. On its back were three squashed wrecks.

The truck pulled away, and we ran toward the entrance. Mr. Singh was standing at the gate.

"Hello!" I yelled.

Mr. Singh didn't answer. He gave me a strange look.

"How are you—?" I stopped mid-sentence as a man in a suit stepped out of the guardhouse. He walked over to a large, fancy black car and climbed in.

"Keep moving," I said to Simon.

"What?" he asked.

I grabbed him by the arm. "Just keep moving, don't look at Mr. Singh and don't say anything to him."

The car started up and passed through the gates as we walked by, missing us by only a foot or two.

"Watch it, buddy!" Simon yelled. "Learn how to drive, you jerk!"

The windows were up, so the driver didn't hear Simon any more than he noticed us. I pulled Simon ahead a few more feet until the car drove off, disappearing into traffic, and then we spun back around.

"Thank you for doing that," Mr. Singh said. "That is the boss."

"The guy who owns this place?" I asked.

"Yes, the guy who now owns the land and is building the condos," Mr. Singh explained. "He would not be happy if he knew I was letting you into the yard."

"I don't want to get you in trouble. Sorry."

"No need to apologize. You need to get into the yard to feed your cats. It is a risk I am willing to take."

"And if he caught you?" I asked.

Mr. Singh shrugged. "He would fire me, I think. He is not such a nice man."

"Or such a great driver," Simon added.

"I have spoken to him. I believe that he would run over any*body* or any*thing* that got in the way of this project," Mr. Singh said.

"Even the cats," I said.

"He does not know anything about the colony of cats."

"And if he did know?" I asked.

"It would make no difference. It might even be worse for the cats."

"How could it be worse?" I asked.

"He might do something to them. He is only caring about the money. All I can do is buy a little more time. They are moving the wrecks. It is my decision which cars and which parts of the yard are cleared first. I will keep them away from the colony." He paused. "At least for a week or two."

"That's better than nothing," Simon said. "It gives us time to do something."

"You have a plan?" Mr. Singh asked.

I shook my head. "Nothing. Do you?" I asked.

"Nothing. I just hope if we allow the cats enough time, perhaps they will find another place to live for themselves."

"With that big fence around the place, can they even get out?" Simon asked.

I hadn't even thought of that.

"It is too high for them to climb, but there are places where there is a space at the bottom where they could escape," Mr. Singh said.

"If they knew they *had* to escape. I wish I could tell them what was happening. I wish they understood how much danger they are in," I said.

"And it is big danger. They will be injured, crushed, killed when the cars are moved. I wish…" Mr. Singh's voice trailed off. "But we must not give up hope. Where there is life, there is hope."

"You're right," I agreed. Only I didn't know how long there was going to be any life in the junkyard.

Twenty-One

I looked at my watch. It was still early. Early enough for me to avoid "the boss," who didn't show up in the mornings. Early enough for Mr. Singh to let me into the yard so I could feed the cats and still get to school on time.

I strolled along the outside of the fence. The advertisements for the condos were still bright and fresh. I wished somebody had taken a can of spray paint and covered them up. Wait, if I got a can, I could do it. Nobody would know about the condos, so nobody would buy them. But it wouldn't stop the condos from going up, and it might get me in big trouble. Besides, I'd promised my mother I wouldn't do anything stupid. Spray-painting a fence was stupid, and useless, which made for a bad combination. If it was stupid but could lead to something positive, that would be different.

I looked up and jumped. Hunter was standing on the top of the fence, looking down at me.

"It's good to know the fence isn't too high for you," I said.

He crouched down and continued to look at me.

"Your foot must be almost perfect now," I said.

He lifted his front paw to show me it was...no, it was the other foot, the one that wasn't hurt, that he raised. He wasn't showing me his foot was better after all. That was just wishful thinking on my part.

But, wait, he *was* holding up the good one, so that meant the foot he had hurt was supporting his weight. Maybe he *was* showing me it was better. Dr. Reynolds would think I was nuts if I told him that, but still.

"I'm glad it's better," I said. "I bet that fence is too high for King to climb. He'd be like Humpty Dumpty if he fell."

I walked over until I was right beneath him. He stayed seated.

"I've got some food," I said. "I just wish I had a solution. I'm trying to come up with an answer. I just don't have it yet. But I do have something you'll like."

I opened up the bag I was carrying and pulled out a piece of sweet-and-sour pork, left over from Simon's dinner the night before. I reached up, and Hunter bent down and gently took the piece of meat from my fingers.

"I've got some more of this," I said. "Plus, I have some other stuff. How about if I meet you inside?"

He swallowed the tidbit I'd given him and jumped off the top of the fence, disappearing inside, as if he'd understood what I'd said.

I came around the corner cautiously. The gate was just ahead, and Mr. Singh was standing out front. I didn't yell or wave. I had to make sure he was alone. When he saw me, he waved me over.

"Good morning, Taylor," he said. "This is a good time to go inside. There is nobody here yet."

"Do you think the boss will be here soon?" I asked.

"Not him. Not until noon. But soon the trucks will start arriving, probably within the hour. Come, please."

He led me in through the gate and locked it behind us.

The whole front area had already been cleared out completely. Where there once had been old parts, machinery pieces and car skeletons, all that remained was the crushed- and chipped-brick-covered ground.

"It's so empty. I can't believe how fast they're removing things," I said.

"They are taking everything away quickly. They cannot start excavating the site until everything is gone."

"Excavating?" I asked.

"Digging. They must dig down deep before they can build up high," he explained. "The new boss keeps saying 'Time is money' and yells at everybody to work faster. I do not think I want to work for him."

"You're going to quit?"

"Oh, no, I will not leave here now, but he has offered me a job," he said.

"A job? Wait, I'm sorry. I've been so wrapped up in what was going to happen to the cats, I hadn't thought about what would happen to you when this place closes. I'm so sorry."

"The boss offered me the job of security while the construction takes place, and when it is a condominium, they will need security too."

"So you could keep your job."

"I would prefer to work elsewhere. Besides, he wishes for me to work evenings and weekends. He has scheduled me to work *this* weekend."

"I know you like to spend that time with your family," I said.

He shrugged. "I will stay until the cars are gone, and until the cats are gone."

"How long is that going to take?" I asked. "How long do the cats have?"

"I can continue to direct them to other parts of the yard for this week, but soon there will be no other areas to clear, and they will begin taking the cars of the colony away."

"So, this week, but not much longer?" I asked.

He nodded his head.

We walked to the colony clearing. Surrounded by the familiar wrecks, it was as if nothing had changed. There were a dozen cats lying down, sitting, walking and sleeping.

"Do you think they even know what's happening?" I asked.

"They can tell by the sounds and smells that something is happening. But they do not know what."

"Maybe it's better they don't know since there's nothing we can do. It's like I'm coming here to feed them their last meals," I said.

"Have you thought that maybe you could borrow that trap again, the one you used to catch Hunter, and remove some of the cats?" he asked.

"I could only remove a few, and then what would I do with them? It isn't like they can stay in my apartment."

"I just know they cannot stay here," Mr. Singh said. "But I am sure for some of the cats it will still be okay."

"Do you really believe that?"

"Your Hunter cat, he is very strong and agile. He will get away from the yard, find another place to live," he suggested.

"But what about the other cats?"

"I think it is not so good for them. Did you not tell me there are other colonics of cats?" he asked.

"There are lots, but that doesn't mean they can find them. Some are on the other side of the city. There's no way they could get there, at least not by themselves. If only there was some way."

"Do you have an idea?" he asked me.

"Not an idea. Not even the beginning of an idea," I said. "You said you were going to be working this weekend?"

"Two twelve-hour shifts."

"So I could come and see the cats, right?" I asked.

"You may come and see the cats *and* the security guard," he said.

"Thanks. It'll be good to see all of you," I said. While I still can, I thought, but didn't say.

"You are always so good to bring food for the cats," he said. "You are a good boy."

"Thanks."

I opened up the bag, and the cats all became interested in me. I pulled out a few of the scraps and tossed them to the ground. I didn't see Hunter anywhere. I guess he hadn't understood what I'd said about meeting me inside for more food. Either that or he didn't care for sweet-and-sour pork.

Twenty-Two

I looked down at the math questions. It was like they were written in a language I didn't understand. I should have understood. Mr. Spence had explained how to do them, and he was a good teacher. I just couldn't follow the lesson. My mind kept drifting off, thinking about my cats.

I looked over at Simon. His head was down, eyes on his paper, as his pencil raced through the questions. No surprise. I'd ask him to explain the questions to me right after school—well, right after I stopped in at the junkyard. No, I couldn't stop in after school. There would be too many trucks, and the boss could be there. I couldn't wait until it closed to sneak in either, because of the new fence. Maybe I could climb over the fence. There wasn't any barbed wire, and it would be dark but not that dark. Maybe I should get Simon to come and feed the cats instead of helping me with my math questions.

"Taylor?"

I looked up. Mr. Spence was standing over my desk. He looked concerned.

"Taylor, it's recess."

The room was almost deserted, and the last of the kids were heading out the door. I was so preoccupied I hadn't even noticed. Simon lingered for a few seconds at the door and nodded my way before heading out.

"Are you all right?" he asked.

"I'm just working on my math questions," I said.

He reached down and spun the paper around to look at my answers, or lack of answers.

"I'm having a little trouble," I said.

"Nothing you can't overcome, you know that," he said. "We can work on it later. I can explain it again, help you. Are you sure you're okay?"

"I guess I was just concentrating," I said. That wasn't a lie. I was concentrating, just not on the questions.

"Concentrating on the math?" he asked.

I *could* have lied, but I didn't want to lie to him. "No, sir, I was thinking about a problem with the cats."

"What sort of problem?" he asked.

"The junkyard is being redeveloped into condos," I explained.

"But where will the cats live?" he asked.

"I don't know, and that's the problem."

"And you're worried about what's going to become of them," he said.

"Really worried. I don't know what to do."

"You keep thinking. Maybe something will happen to make it better," he said.

"I wish it would."

"But for right now, why don't you go out, take a break and enjoy recess."

"Thanks, sir." I got up, pushed my chair in and started for the door.

"Taylor," Mr. Spence called out, and I stopped. "I'll think about your problem too," he said. "Just remember, the more people who think about it, the better the chance of somebody coming up with an answer."

I nodded.

I hurried outside and looked for my friends. They were standing together outside the door.

"Hey, guys," I said.

"We've been thinking," Simon said.

"About the cats," Devon added.

"We've all been trying to think of a way to save them," Jaime continued.

"And?" I asked hopefully.

"And we haven't been able to come up with an answer," Rupinder replied.

"But we are still trying to think of something," Alexander added. He put a hand on my shoulder. "Nobody is giving up yet. Maybe we'll come up with something in a day or two."

"If we don't come up with something soon, it's all over," I said. "I wish it was as simple as moving them someplace else."

"Well, why don't we do that?" Simon asked.

"Why don't we do what?" I asked.

"Move them someplace else," he said.

"Yeah, right, like I could move fifty cats," I scoffed.

"Not you," Simon said. "*Us*."

"All of us," Devon said, and Jaime, Rupinder, Mohammad and Alexander nodded in agreement.

"We would be like the United Nations," Jaime added.

I was thinking more like Catboy, the Korean Kid and assorted other superheroes.

"Even if we work together, how do we trap them or move them, and where would we move them to?" I questioned. "Seven kids are better than one, but we're still only seven kids."

"How about Dr. Reynolds?" Simon said. "He'd help, wouldn't he?"

Yeah, he *would* help, I thought.

"You told me he has traps, and what about those wild cat people? Wouldn't they help too?" Simon asked.

"I hadn't thought about that," I said. "But even once we trapped them, where would we move them to?"

"There are other colonies around the city, right?" Simon asked.

"That's what Dr. Reynolds and Doris told me," I agreed. "They said there are hundreds."

"Well, maybe it isn't just you who can move from one home to another, but the cats can too," Simon said.

"We've all moved," Alexander said. "Some of us from one country to another."

"One *continent* to another," Rupinder added.

"So tell me, why can't the cats be moved to a new colony?" Jaime questioned. "Moving worked for all of us."

"I guess they could," I agreed.

"Well, then maybe we have a plan," Simon said.

"Maybe we do." I paused. "Thanks, guys."

"Are you feeling better now?" Jaime asked.

"Yeah, I am, a little." Now all I had to do was convince Dr. Reynolds to help us. Without him, we had a plan that had no chance of working.

Twenty-Three

I sat in the waiting room, doing the only thing I could—wait. Everybody else had a dog or cat or even a guinea pig with them. I just had me—me and an idea, and not even an appointment to discuss that idea. Suddenly I started to get even more nervous.

The door opened, and a woman and her daughter, who was about my age, came out leading a gigantic dog, an Irish setter. It was bouncing and pulling at its leash, and it took the two of them to stop it from dragging them right out the front door.

Dr. Reynolds poked his head out of the examination room and saw me. "Taylor?" he called out. "What are you doing here?"

I got up. "Can I talk to you for a minute?"

"I'm sort of busy. Can it wait until tonight? You could call me."

"I know you're busy, but I really hoped I could talk to you in person. I can wait until you're through with everybody," I suggested. "It's important."

"Now you've got me interested. If you say it's important, I'm sure it is. Come in."

Every eye in the place was on me as I walked into his office. He closed the door behind us.

"Is this about Hunter?" he asked.

"It's about all of the cats, the whole colony. They're in danger."

He took on a serious look. "Poison, disease, mange? What's wrong?"

"They're redeveloping the junkyard. It's being turned into condominiums," I explained.

"That's awful. The cats that don't die during construction will be put out on the streets. Most of them won't survive."

"I know. That's why I want to talk to you. You said there were other colonies in the city, right?"

"There are spots all over the city, but none of them are close enough for the cats to migrate to," he said. "Even if they knew where to go, the nearest site that could accommodate that many cats is too far away."

"But it could fit that many cats?"

"The Leslie Spit could hold hundreds of feral cats, but there's no point in thinking about it. It's on the other side of the city. Even if they knew where they were going, I don't think a cat could survive that trip. Plus, there's no way a whole colony could make it. It's not like you can *herd* cats."

"But you could *carry* them," I said.

Dr. Reynolds looked even more curious.

"We could trap them in cages and drive them over," I explained.

"How would you even get that many traps and cages?" he asked.

"That's one of the things I wanted to ask you about. *You* have traps. *You* have cages."

"Not enough cages to hold fifty cats. That is about the size of the colony, isn't it?"

I nodded in agreement.

"I don't have that many cages or traps!"

"But I bet you know people who have some."

"Yes, I know people who have cages and traps. We could probably find that many cages. But even if we could gather the cages, do you know how hard it would be to trap the entire colony?" he asked.

"Really hard."

"More than hard, it would be close to impossible. It could take weeks and weeks to trap that many cats."

"We don't have weeks. We only have this weekend," I said, looking at the floor.

"In that case, it *is* impossible."

"Maybe it is. But if we don't try, they're all going to die. Or almost all of them, especially the little ones and probably the older ones. Maybe we can't trap them all, but we can trap some of them. We could save some of them, couldn't we?"

He didn't answer right away. I took that as a good sign. He must be thinking about what I'd suggested. Either that or thinking of a nice way to turn me down without saying I was crazy.

"So let me get this straight," he said. "You want me to try to round up fifty or so cages and traps."

"Fifty would do."

"You then want me to go with you—"

"And other people," I said. "We won't be alone."

"Fine, I'll go with you and other people to the junk-yard and try to trap the whole colony of cats, maybe fifty cats, in two days. Then we're going to drive them across town and release them, so they can rebuild their colony in a whole new place. Is that what you're suggesting?"

It was, but it made less sense when he put it all out there in front of us.

"I guess so."

"Even though you know it's basically impossible and it's just going to be a waste of our time. Is that what you want me to be part of?" he asked. "Is that what you want me to spend my *entire* weekend doing?"

I nodded.

"Okay, as long as I understand the plan." He paused, and then he smiled. "I'm game. What time do you want me there?"

Twenty-Four

We stood in the alley beside the junkyard. The place where Mr. Singh had told me we should wait. There was a small army of us. Hopefully a small army would be enough people. There was Dr. Reynolds and my mother, of course, but we had other help. I'd brought the *United Nations* along—Simon, Devon, Mohammad, Rupinder, Alexander and Jaime. Maybe *brought* wasn't the right word. I couldn't have kept them away if I had tried. They wanted to help the cats as much as I did.

Dr. Reynolds had also brought along some people from the Feral Cat Association. One of them, Doris, I'd met before. The other four—two older men, a woman about my mother's age and a guy in his teens—were very friendly, talkative and excited to be there. They all really wanted to help.

Dr. Reynolds had also brought an array of equipment. He had the traps as well as fifty cages to transfer the cats to after we had trapped them. He'd also brought along thick work gloves for everybody, a couple of big nets and medication to tranquilize the trapped cats that got too wild, so they wouldn't hurt themselves. He also had four long poles. At the end of two of them were snares—loops that could fit around a cat's neck and drag it out. On the end of the other two were hypodermic needles so they could be tranquilized and then removed. It felt like we were going on a safari.

Now all we needed was a way inside the junkyard. We couldn't go in the front gates. Two days ago they'd installed security cameras to watch all the vehicles coming and going. There was no way we could get all these people, the equipment and the vans in without being seen. But Mr. Singh had told me he'd find a way for us to get in.

"Mr. Singh will let us in soon," I said. I'd said it loud enough for those around me to hear but also to reassure myself. I figured he was going to cut a small opening in the fence for us to climb through.

I knew I wasn't the only person who was getting antsy. I'd overheard snippets of conversation. People were nervous about going into the yard and doing this, especially since I'd told them what Mr. Singh had said— the new owner was going to contact the police and charge anybody who trespassed on the property.

Strangely, though, I think people were more nervous that we *wouldn't* be able to move the cats. It would be awful if all these people and the equipment we'd assembled weren't able to get inside. But that wouldn't happen. I knew I could count on Mr. Singh, unless something had happened.

What if the boss had showed up, or they put on extra guards or additional security cameras? I hadn't been inside the yard for two days—aside from the security cameras being in place, there was too much work going on inside for me to visit. Maybe they had moved more quickly than we expected and had already removed the cars from the colony's area. But Mr. Singh would have let me know if that had happened, if he had known how to get in touch with me. If it all happened last night or this morning, he wouldn't have had any way to tell me.

An engine started on the other side of the fence. I was right, they were moving the wrecks today. There was an enormous crash and a section of the fence exploded, splintering and flying into the air in a cloud of dust, dirt and debris. Out of the cloud emerged a gray forklift with Mr. Singh at the controls! And on top of his brilliant red turban sat a large yellow hard hat.

The machine rumbled into the alley and came to a stop. Mr. Singh looked around, trying to see through the cloud of dust that surrounded him. I jumped up and ran over, and the rest of the crowd followed.

"That is some cool ride," Simon yelled.

"It is not a BMW, but it is pretty fancy," Mr. Singh joked. "Is this hole big enough?"

"I should be able to squeeze my van through," Dr. Reynolds said.

"Oh, no need for squeezing. I will make it bigger."

"Please, don't go to any trouble. It should be okay," Dr. Reynolds said.

"It is no trouble, sir," Mr. Singh said. "Have any of you ever driven a forklift through a fence?"

I thought that was a strange question.

"It is a very, very much fun thing to do! I will show you!" Mr. Singh exclaimed.

He started up the engine, and we all backed away. He spun the forklift around like it was a bumper car at the carnival.

Mr. Singh drove forward and crashed the forklift into another section of the fence, and wood and metal fell to the ground. It was like he was unpeeling the junkyard as more and more of the fence disappeared beneath the forklift. He continued until the hole was large enough to drive a transport truck through, sideways. He shut the engine off and jumped down with a big smile on his face.

"I figure since I am fired, I might as well enjoy myself," Mr. Singh explained.

"You're going to get fired?" I exclaimed.

"Most certainly! What sort of security guard would allow somebody to take down a section of the fence he was guarding? But please, it only saves me from quitting!"

I was wrong. It was more like a military campaign than a safari we were on. Dr. Reynolds placed traps around the heart of the colony. Each of the traps was baited with salmon and chicken chunks.

It hadn't taken long for the first catches. Within an hour of the traps being set and us backing away, we'd caught the first cat, followed quickly by the second, third and fourth. We brought the cats back to the van and transferred them to holding cages and then returned the traps to the colony.

As Dr. Reynolds had suggested, we hadn't fed the cats for the past three days. Our best tool was their hunger. The new fence kept most of the cats from leaving the yard to find food, and a lot of the rodents in the yard had been scared away by the trucks and activity. The cats were so hungry, they couldn't resist the traps.

I heard a metallic thud and knew we had caught another cat. I slipped on my gloves. By the time I circled around the wrecks to where I thought the sound had come from, there were already people at the trap. Simon and Doris were both peering in. I hurried to their side.

It was another one of the teen cats, one of Miss Mittens's kittens, who were not so small anymore. That made me happy. If we caught one of her kittens, then maybe we could catch her. So far I hadn't even seen her, or Hunter, or some of the others, including King. I wondered if the mouth of the trap would even be big enough to let King in. If he was caught, it would take a crane to move him to the truck.

"Let me take that," Dr. Reynolds said. He picked the cage up. The cat hissed and snarled and bumped against the bars, trying to get away from him. "It's okay, kitty, nobody is going to hurt you," he said.

I don't think the cat believed him. "This makes five. We've already got ten percent of the colony," I said. "At this rate we'll have them all within ten hours."

He picked up the cage. "It would be nice if it worked that way, but I'm afraid it doesn't."

"Sure it does," I said. "One hour for ten percent, so that means ten hours for one hundred percent."

"I'm not questioning your math," he said.

I followed him back to the van.

"It will get progressively harder to catch cats as we go on. The first ones we caught are the younger, less cautious ones."

He opened up the back of the van, and the cats jumped against the bars of their cages, trying to get away from us. He placed the trap against an empty cage and opened the doors of both. A few shakes and the cat slipped through the opening of the trap and into the cage. Dr. Reynolds closed the cage, picked up the empty trap and closed the van's doors.

"My guess is that for Hunter and King we're going to have to use the snares or the nets," Dr. Reynolds said. "That's probably the only way we're going to get a cat like Hunter, especially since he's already been in a trap. He won't make the same mistake twice."

I knew Dr. Reynolds was right. I'd been thinking the same thing. If we were able to catch every cat in the colony except one, it would be Hunter. I tried to ease my guilt by thinking that if any of the cats could survive without the colony, it would be him.

The thought made me feel a little better, but not much. I'd taken him away from the colony, and now I was taking the colony away from him, cat by cat. But what choice did I have?

Twenty-Five

I moved among the wrecks, squeezing through tight spaces, trying to avoid sharp edges and rusty bits. Before we had entered the yard that morning, I was afraid the owner might have removed too many cars and gotten too close to the colony. Now, with the cats using the remaining wrecks to hide, I wished there were fewer cars, so the cats wouldn't have so many places to hide.

I trailed behind Dr. Reynolds. We each carried one of the pole snares. We'd seen an occasional flash of fur and heard movement in the wrecks, but the remaining cats were very elusive. Twice I thought I saw Hunter, but a glimpse of black amid shadows wasn't much of a confirmation.

I was really surprised King hadn't surfaced. He was so big and slow moving I didn't think he could run or hide, but somehow he'd managed to stay hidden. He was always so front and center when it came to food, I figured he'd be the first to enter a trap. Maybe he wasn't as desperate as some of the other cats because he was so fat and could live off his blubber for days.

Hunter remaining hidden was to be expected, but I hadn't seen Miss Mittens either. She had never been timid or reserved. We'd trapped all four of her kittens, although they really weren't kittens anymore.

Maybe, with her kittens all grown up, Miss Mittens had more time to spend with Hunter. I pictured the two of them together, like the scene in *Lady and the Tramp* where they are sitting in an alley sharing a plate of pasta. That was why Miss Mittens and Hunter weren't here now. Obviously I was suffering from more of that anthromorphing thing.

"Got you!" Dr. Reynolds yelled.

His pole was stuck in a hole in the wreckage. Part of me hoped it was Hunter on the other end, but part of me hoped it wasn't.

Dr. Reynolds dragged the pole out of the crevice. Whatever was on the other end seemed to be putting up a good fight, like Hunter or King would. He pulled the end clear. It was Sherpa! Rupinder would be so happy, although Sherpa certainly wasn't. He was spitting and digging in his claws, trying to get free.

"This is a little like fishing," Dr. Reynolds said. "I just wish we could let them know it's catch and release."

He pulled the pole closer until Sherpa was right there, only a foot or two from his hands.

"What a beautiful cat," Dr. Reynolds said. "Himalayan cats are among my favorites."

"His name is Sherpa," I said.

Sherpa's eyes were wild with fear. Dr. Reynolds held the pole with one hand and reached for the cat with the other. Sherpa attacked him, landing three or four fast strikes harmlessly against his heavy gloves and jacket.

"Can't blame you, big guy," he said. "I'd be fighting too." He turned to me. "Can you get me a cage?"

"Oh, yeah! Sure, of course."

I dropped my pole and ran to get a cage. There weren't many left because most were filled with cats. We had thirty-four, no, thirty-five now with Sherpa.

By the time I returned, Dr. Reynolds had Sherpa pinned to the ground under a big gloved hand. I opened the cage and he picked the cat up by the scruff of the neck, the way its mother would have picked it up. Sherpa relaxed, maybe remembering his mother, and Dr. Reynolds placed him in the cage. The second Dr. Reynolds released his hold on Sherpa, the cat sprang to life, clawing the bars to try and get free.

Dr. Reynolds picked up the cage, and we headed for the van again. "We're doing well, but we don't have much daylight left," he said.

I looked at my watch and knew he was right. It was almost four o'clock. We'd spent the entire day at the junkyard. It would be dark in less than an hour, and it was starting to get cold.

Throughout the course of the day, we'd been losing our helpers. First Doris, then one of the men, and then Alexander, Jaime and Rupinder had to leave. I wished Rupinder were here to know we'd caught Sherpa, but I'd call him when I got home. I understood people had things they had to do. I was just grateful they'd been here to help for some of the time.

"We're going to have to call it a day soon," Dr. Reynolds said.

"But there are still fifteen cats to catch," I said.

"We still have tomorrow morning. But to be honest, we've done a lot better than I thought we would."

"But not as good as we're going to do," I added.

As we approached the van, I heard the cats. Some of them were wailing loudly. Dr. Reynolds opened the back door and the cats got even louder. Some of them sat in the corner of their cage, but others were bouncing around, desperately trying to get out.

"What happens to them all tonight?" I asked.

He closed the van door. "I'm going to give them all an examination, as best I can, give them their shots, make sure they have food and water, and possibly tranquilize some of the more agitated ones so they don't harm themselves."

"That's a lot of work."

"With any luck I'll be finished by midnight."

"And then you'll come back here tomorrow morning?"

"Bright and early, but you know, this is why I became a vet. I really have to thank you," Dr. Reynolds said.

"Thank *me*?" I questioned. "I have to thank *you*!"

"Doing this is my thanks. I never would have tried to move the cats if you hadn't been so insistent."

"What choice did we have?" I asked.

"We could have assumed we couldn't do anything and just let the cats survive or not survive. Sometimes it's easier to turn away than act. Thanks for not letting me turn away."

"None of this would have been possible without you, and your friends," I said.

"And *your* friends," he said. "It was great to have all that help."

"They're all willing to come help tomorrow too."

"That's great, but I think the best way they could help would be if they don't come tomorrow."

"I don't understand," I said.

"The noise and commotion of extra people is starting to work against us. Think about Hunter. The cats we haven't caught are the most reclusive or timid or careful ones. The fewer of us here tomorrow, the more likely we'll be able to catch the remaining cats."

"That makes sense."

"I'll ask Doris to come. The two of us, plus you and your mother, would probably be enough."

"Could Simon come as well? He's been here from the beginning."

"Okay, Simon too," he agreed. "We probably couldn't keep him away anyway, could we?"

"Probably not," I agreed. "I think my other friends are going to be disappointed though."

"Tell them they can be there when we release the cats," he suggested. "That's a lot more fun anyway."

"They'd like that," I said. "I'll call them when I get home."

"And that should happen right now. I have a lot of things to do with the cats before I can call it a night."

"Great. We'll be here bright and early tomorrow, right?" I said.

"How bright and early?" he asked.

"How about six?"

"How about eight?"

"Seven is in the middle," I countered.

"And seven thirty is when it's light enough to see."

"Okay, seven thirty. Deal."

Twenty-Six

It hadn't just gotten colder overnight. It had snowed. It was more a dusting than a full snowfall, but it covered the ground with a fine layer. It actually made the alley and junkyard look fresh and pretty. If the junkyard was going to send a Christmas card, this would have been the picture on the front of it. Of course the junkyard didn't send Christmas cards, and by the time Christmas did arrive in three weeks, there wouldn't be a junkyard. I was willing to bet the condo development wouldn't send a Christmas card either.

I stomped my feet to drive the cold out of them. We'd agreed not to enter the yard until we were all here. So we were waiting for Dr. Reynolds. In fairness, we were early, so it wasn't like he was late. I wondered how late it had been when he finally finished with the cats the night before. I wished I could have been there to help.

Mr. Spence had mentioned to us more than once that you start preparing for your career when you're in grade school. I was thinking more and more that I wanted to be a vet, so I guess I was preparing.

"I hope he gets here soon," I said, breaking the silence.

"I hope it gets warmer," my mother added.

"That would be good. I'd like it if the snow melted," Simon said.

"No, the snow is good," I said.

"How do you figure that?" Simon asked.

"The cats will have left tracks, so we can see where they've gone."

"That just means we'll be able to see what we can't catch," Simon said.

"We'll catch them," I said.

"We'll catch *some* of them," he replied.

"We'll catch all of them, if we have to be here all day and all night," I said.

"Count me in for the day part," Simon replied.

"I'm sure that's all the time we'll need," my mother added. "I'm sure we'll catch them all by then."

The van came bumping slowly down the alley. Dr. Reynolds was at the wheel, and Doris was in the passenger seat. Before they even came to a stop, I could hear the other "passengers." The cats didn't sound any happier than they had the previous night. Doris and Dr. Reynolds climbed out.

"Good morning!" Dr. Reynolds said. "How is everybody doing?"

"We're good," I said. "How did the examinations go? Are the cats healthy?"

"Healthy and noisy," said Dr. Reynolds. "Let's go in."

We stepped over the remains of the fence and entered the yard. I checked the ground, looking for tracks, but there were no prints in the snow. If there had been any, they had already been covered by the snow.

"Do you think there'll be any in the traps?" I asked. We'd left the remaining nine traps baited when we went home the night before.

"We can only hope," he said.

We didn't have long to wait. Two more cats were in traps. One of them was Alexander's Russian Blue, Kot! I wished Alexander were here to see it. He'd be so thrilled to release him later that day.

I'd given my friends a call after I got home the previous evening. Devon's dad was going to drive them to the place where the cats were going to be released.

"I'm sorry Hunter isn't one of the cats we caught," my mother said.

"But still, we have two more cats," I said.

"Do you think Hunter's even in the junkyard?" Simon asked.

"I don't know, but I didn't see any tracks leading out of here this morning." I was trying to reassure myself more than I was trying to convince him.

"That could mean he didn't come back here last night. If I was him, or any of these cats, I'd be trying to find someplace else to live, and fast," Simon said.

"Not likely," Dr. Reynolds said. He picked up the cage with Kot in it. Kot hissed angrily at him. "Most animals retreat farther into their dens when they're threatened. So rather than running away, they retreat and wait it out."

"So you think he's still here?" I asked.

"I guess we'll soon find out. Can you two bring the cats back to the van?" he asked.

"Of course," I said.

"No problem," Simon offered.

"You can leave them in their traps rather than transfer them to cages," he added. "We'll have enough traps to finish up what we need to do."

The cats got frightened when we picked them up, and Kot hurled himself against the side of the cage, almost causing me to drop it.

"I wish we could tell them it's going to be all right," I said. "That we're doing this for their own good."

"If we could do that, we wouldn't have needed to do any of this," Simon offered. "The cats could have left on their own."

"I guess you're right," I said.

We opened the back door of the van, triggering an avalanche of howls and cries from the cats inside. Most of them had calmed down overnight, but the drive had some of them upset again.

"Just bringing a couple of your friends," I said as we placed the two traps in the van and closed the door.

"Look who's over there!" Simon shouted.

I spun around excitedly, expecting Hunter, but it was Rocky. The big raccoon was waddling down the alley toward us. He looked up and saw us, but he didn't slow down or change directions.

"Maybe we should get out of the way," Simon suggested. "I wouldn't want to, you know, *frighten* him."

I laughed. "I'm sure he's *terrified* of you!"

Rocky reached the place where the fence had been knocked over. He sat down and picked up a piece of the shattered fence with his front paws. He held it up as if he was examining it. His gaze shot back and forth from the piece in his hands to the larger pieces on the ground.

"He looks like he's trying to figure out what happened," Simon said.

"He *is* trying to figure it out. Raccoons are very smart."

"I read that, but if he was really smart he would have read the advertisement for the new condos and warned the colony," Simon suggested.

"Maybe he did, but they didn't listen, because I know that Rocky is particularly smart." I took a couple of steps toward him.

"Mr. Singh knocked down the fence!" I called out. "He used a forklift."

Rocky looked at me. I didn't know if he understood, but he was listening.

"He did it so we could trap all the cats. We're not going to do anything bad with them. We're trying to relocate the colony," I said. I thought he might need an explanation as to why all of this was happening. "You know, with the condos coming and everything, we have to move them."

"I thought he'd already read that," Simon said.

I ignored Simon and sat down on the pavement so Rocky and I were practically eye to eye, separated by only a dozen feet or so.

"Taylor, what are you doing?" Simon demanded. "He could bite you or something."

"I'm okay," I said over my shoulder.

Rocky stared at me intently. He studied me the way he'd been studying the fence.

"I wanted to talk to you about Hunter," I said. "Maybe you don't know him by that name. He's the big black cat with the white patch on his forehead that looks like a star," I said, pointing to my forehead.

Rocky looked thoughtful.

"You know him. He's your buddy, the cat you share meals with sometimes."

I could have sworn Rocky nodded his head. I couldn't help but laugh, and in response I thought Rocky smiled.

"I need to find Hunter," I said. "If he stays here, he might die."

Rocky stopped smiling.

"If you can show me where he is, I can trap him and take him to the new place. He'll be safe. We need to bring him along."

"Taylor, he's a raccoon," Simon called out.

I turned around. Simon was looking at me like I was crazy.

"I know what *type* of animal he is," I said. "And I also know we have to find Hunter. Do you have a better idea how to do that?"

He shrugged. "I guess not."

I turned back to Rocky. "I know Hunter could probably survive, find another place around here to live. And I know you'd miss him, but those other cats, they're going to need him. Without him, some of them, especially the younger ones, won't make it." I paused. "They need him, and I need you to help me find him. Please."

Rocky didn't move. He sat there with a studious look on his face. If he were a person, I would have been sure he understood and was thinking about what I'd said, deciding if he should trust me, deciding whether or not to take me to Hunter. But he wasn't a person.

"Do you want me to try it in Korean?" Simon asked.

"What?"

"Do you want me to try to explain it to him in Korean?" Simon repeated.

"What makes you think he can understand Korean?" I asked.

"What makes you think he can understand English? Taylor, he doesn't understand *any* languages. He's a *raccoon*."

"If he did understand a language, it would be English. That's the language that's all around him."

"Maybe if he was a chubby guy in a fur coat with a mask he would, but he's an animal."

"Are you saying dogs don't understand things? Commands, orders, things like *sit* or *come* or *fetch* or—"

Rocky abruptly got up and rambled into the junkyard.

"Where do you think he's going?" Simon asked.

"I guess there's only one way to find out," I said.

Twenty-Seven

Rocky waddled quickly. We had to trot to keep up. I was surprised by how fast he was able to go. He was headed straight for the colony. I had to fight the urge to yell to Simon *I told you so*, but I knew it wouldn't have been very nice. Besides, it wasn't like Rocky had led us anywhere or to anyone, yet. He could be headed for the only part of the yard that still had cars and shelter.

He had almost reached the first of the remaining wrecks, so I picked up my pace. I didn't want to lose sight of him. Despite my best efforts, he rounded the wreck and vanished. Instantly there was a loud scream— my mother's.

I raced around the corner. She was standing on top of a car with a cage in her hands.

"That raccoon!" she exclaimed, pointing. "It almost ran me over!"

"Up there?" I exclaimed.

"No, no, down there. He ran right by me."

"How did you get up there?" Simon asked.

"I jumped, one jump. It just came out of nowhere and—"

"I have to follow him!" I yelled, taking off after Rocky.

He ran through the center of the colony. Dr. Reynolds and Doris were on the edge of the clearing and saw him. He was hard to miss. With Simon at my side, I ran after Rocky, who had now reached the far side of the clearing and disappeared between two rows of wrecks.

Dr. Reynolds met us as we approached the gap Rocky had slipped through.

"That is one gigantic raccoon!" Dr. Reynolds exclaimed.

"That's Rocky," I explained.

I started after him again, but Dr. Reynolds reached out and grabbed my arm. "I think we better give him a wide berth. Raccoons can be dangerous, especially when they're cornered."

"No, you don't understand," I said. "We have to follow him. He's taking us to Hunter."

Dr. Reynolds either didn't understand or didn't believe me—but why would he?

"Really, he is," I exclaimed. "I have to follow him or we may never find Hunter. You have to believe me. You have to *trust* me."

He let go of my arm. "I lead. You follow."

"And I'll wait right here," Simon offered.

I knew Simon wasn't convinced of any of this, but what could I expect? It didn't make much sense.

Dr. Reynolds started down a narrow path. Wherever Rocky had gone, he wasn't in sight. There were so many little side passages, nooks and crannies where he could have disappeared. We'd just have to search.

I was grateful Dr. Reynolds was with me. Not just because it meant another set of eyes, but it was a little scary to be in here following a gigantic raccoon. Just because I'd given him a name didn't mean he wasn't a wild animal—a big wild animal—and I was following him through a junkyard.

"There he is," Dr. Reynolds whispered softly.

He was sitting in the shadows of a big truck piled on the top of a crushed car. And in the shadows, tucked beneath the car, was a hole. Was that Rocky's den? Was that his hole? Was he running in there to get away from us? It couldn't be his den. The opening was way too small to allow him in.

With his front paws, Rocky began digging at the little hole, kicking up stones and clumps of frozen dirt.

"What's he doing?" I asked.

"He's digging, but I don't know why. There's no way he can make that hole big enough for himself. Maybe there's food down there he's trying to get at," Dr. Reynolds suggested.

Not food. Hunter. Hunter was down that hole.

Rocky stopped digging, but his face, his entire head, was in the hole.

"I have no idea what he is doing," Dr. Reynolds said.

I did. Hunter was down that hole, and Rocky was talking to him. I knew it. I also knew I couldn't tell Dr. Reynolds that.

Rocky pulled his head out of the hole and looked me in the eye. He let out a little cry, nodded his head slightly, lifted up one front paw and waved. He then turned and ran off, vanishing between the wrecks.

"That was certainly strange," Dr. Reynolds said. "I have never seen a raccoon do something like that. He is *incredibly* big."

"And incredibly *smart*," I added.

I rushed over to the hole and tried to peer down. It was too deep, too dark, to see down to the bottom.

"Hunter is down there," I said. "In this hole."

"You can see him?"

"It's too dark. I can't see anything, but I know he's down there."

Dr. Reynolds didn't argue. But I didn't expect him to. I knew, despite all his scientific training, he believed me.

He came over, pulled a flashlight out of his pocket and shone it down the hole. It *was* deep. Dr. Reynolds moved the flashlight around so the beam would reach the bottom. Eyes reflected back! There were two big bright sets of eyes.

"They're down there!" I exclaimed. "It's Hunter and Miss Mittens!"

"It is," Dr. Reynolds said. "And they're not alone."

"Not alone. There's another cat?"

"Judging from what I can see, not another *cat*, kittens."

"Kittens!"

At the bottom of the hole, surrounding Miss Mittens, were her kittens. I couldn't tell for sure, but I thought there were four of them. "How many do you see?" I asked.

"I believe there are three or even four little pairs of eyes."

"How old do you think they are?" I asked.

"It's hard to tell for sure from this distance, but no more than a couple of weeks old would be my guess."

"Are they okay?" I asked.

"I try not to do my examinations from ten feet away while staring down a hole, but they do look okay, from a distance. I see no reason why they shouldn't be fine," Dr. Reynolds said. "She's a good mother, right?"

"The best," I said proudly.

"Some cats are better parents than others," he said.

"She was good with her last litter," I explained. "I didn't even know she was pregnant again," I added.

"You mentioned you hadn't seen her lately, so I wondered if this might be the case," Dr. Reynolds said. "The mother often stays with them in the den until they're old enough to leave."

"I didn't expect her to have another litter so soon. Her last litter can't be more than six months old."

"Cats can have litters very often. That's why feral cat colonies get so large so quickly. And why we try to neuter them if we can catch them," he added.

"So how do we get them out?" I asked.

"I don't know if we can," Dr. Reynolds said.

"But we can't leave them there. There has to be some way," I argued.

"I'm open to suggestions, but I don't know any way," Dr. Reynolds said.

"Can't you reach them with the snare pole?"

"It's too deep for the pole. Besides, even if I was able to snare them, I'd only be able to get Hunter and Miss Mittens. The kittens are too small and too fragile. I'd kill them if I tried to drag them out."

"What if we tried to dig them out?" I suggested. "We could get a shovel and start digging."

"It's jammed under the wrecks. There's really no place to dig out."

"I could get Mr. Singh to use the forklift to move the wrecks away. I'm sure he has a shovel or two as well."

"I'm afraid moving the wrecks might cause the hole to collapse. Even if that didn't, I'm sure the digging would cause the sides of the hole to cave in and the kittens would be suffocated."

"But if we don't get them out, what will happen to them?"

Dr. Reynolds didn't say anything. He just looked at the ground, which, in a way, was his answer.

Even if the wrecks being removed and the trucks rumbling around the yard didn't cause a cave-in, the cats wouldn't survive once construction started.

"But we have to do something," I said softly.

"I wish there was something we could do," Dr. Reynolds said. "We just have to hope the den can survive long enough for the kittens to become old enough to leave. Hunter will continue to bring them food, and then maybe he can move them elsewhere. From what you've told me, he's a capable cat. If any cat could do it, it would be him."

Dr. Reynolds placed a hand on my shoulder.

I was trying hard not to cry, but I didn't know if I'd be able to hold the tears back.

"Do you think I could be alone?" I asked.

"Of course," Dr. Reynolds said and walked away.

I stared at the ground and down into the hole. Somewhere in the darkness below sat the two cats and their kittens. I knew there was a chance we could catch Hunter. I was certain he was coming out to try to catch food. Maybe we could snag him when he came out next. But without Hunter, the kittens and Miss Mittens would never survive. And if we left them, they were all going to die anyway.

There had to be some way to save them. If only I could talk to Hunter, convince him to bring his family out. I needed to try.

I sat down on the ground. Dr. Reynolds was gone. Good. Talking to Rocky with Simon peering over my shoulder was one thing. Talking to Hunter with Dr. Reynolds listening in was another.

"Hunter, it's me," I said quietly, my voice echoing down the hole. "I know you can hear me."

I took a deep breath. I didn't know if he could hear me, but I wasn't sure what else I could do. I had to say something.

"We've gathered up most of the other cats already. We've got a spot to release all of you. Dr. Reynolds picked it out. It's a good place, but we can't reach you or the kittens. I'm really sorry, but I don't know what else to do."

My voice cracked over the last few words, and I choked back the tears coming to my eyes.

"I don't want to leave you here. I feel awful. I want you to know that...to know I didn't abandon you. I'll come back tomorrow and the next day and the next day if I have to. But if the trucks come, the hole won't hold up. It'll collapse. You'll die. Miss Mittens will die, the kittens will die." I took a deep breath. "We're not giving up. I want you to know that, that's all."

I looked into the hole. I couldn't see anything. What did I expect to see? What did I expect to happen?

I got up and walked toward the clearing, where I knew everybody would be. They were all there, waiting. I brushed away any hint of tears. My mother looked like she might cry too. I guess Dr. Reynolds had told them what we'd found.

"We'll try again tomorrow," she said as she put an arm around my shoulders.

I knew that was the thing to say. But if we couldn't get them out today, would another day be any different? Would the hole even be there tomorrow?

"Look!" Dr. Reynolds called out.

I spun around. Hunter was standing at the edge of the clearing and he was holding something in his mouth. Was it a mouse or a rat—

"It's a kitten," I gasped.

Twenty-Eight

Hunter crept into the clearing, the tiny kitten in his mouth.

"I'll get the snare," Dr. Reynolds whispered.

"No, don't, please."

"But this might be our only chance to catch him," he said.

"We *can't* catch him," I said. "Without him, the kittens won't survive. Miss Mittens won't survive."

"But what is he doing?" my mother asked.

"He's moving the cats someplace safe," Dr. Reynolds said. "Cats will do that when they're threatened. Somehow he's figured out they have to leave."

Hunter had heard and understood me. He knew what had happened. He walked around the edge of the clearing, staying close to the wrecks and as far away from us as possible. It was important we stayed still and tried not to scare him.

Hunter stopped in front of one of the traps. He obviously remembered being in the trap before. I hoped that experience hadn't spooked him so much he wouldn't do what he needed to do.

"It won't hurt you," I whispered. "Just go around it."

"Oh, my goodness," my mother said.

"I can't believe what he's doing," Dr. Reynolds gasped.

Hunter stepped partway into the trap. Not far enough to trigger the door, but far enough to drop the kitten in. He retreated, leaving the kitten, a little ball of black fur, in the trap! It stumbled around, meowing, too small to try to climb out of the trap.

"You don't think that Hunter is, is…He *can't* be," Dr. Reynolds said.

"Yes," I said, answering his unfinished question. "He *is*."

Hunter disappeared. Was he going for a second kitten? He had to be. This wasn't an accident or a mistake.

"This is unbelievable," my mother said. "If he's actually doing what we think he's doing, it's just, just… amazing!"

The words were barely out of her mouth when Hunter appeared with another kitten in his mouth. He walked directly over to the trap, dropped the second kitten into the cage and quickly turned around. The two little kittens huddled together and Hunter disappeared once again.

"I feel like I'm in a Disney movie," Simon said.

"Have you ever heard of anything like this happening before?" my mother asked Dr. Reynolds.

"I've read about wild animals moving their babies out of danger, like away from a forest fire," Dr. Reynolds said. "But this, putting them into a cage...well, I'm seeing it and I hardly believe it." He shook his head. "I'm going to make a point of not telling anyone what I'm seeing today."

"You can tell anybody in the Feral Cat Association," Doris added. "We *all* would believe it."

"Maybe I should go and examine the kittens," he suggested.

"No, not yet," I said. "You don't want to spook Hunter. Wait until he's brought them all out."

"Do you think he's going to bring all of them?" Simon asked.

"I'm counting on it," I said.

Hunter arrived with another kitten in his mouth, and right behind him was Miss Mittens. She was carrying the fourth kitten. She hesitated at the edge of the clearing, but Hunter didn't. He moved straight toward the trap. He dropped the kitten in with the other two. The three of them curled together, crying loudly.

Hunter doubled back to where Miss Mittens was waiting. They touched noses and she followed him back toward the cage.

The kittens' cries became even louder. They sounded desperate. Miss Mittens picked up her pace and trotted straight to the trap. Hunter pressed up against her and sort of nudged her toward the opening.

"Do you see what he's doing?" I whispered.

"I see it, but that doesn't mean I believe it," Dr. Reynolds said.

Miss Mittens stopped beside the cage. I had an image of Hunter giving her a shove. But the kittens had become even louder. She jumped into the cage and the door slammed shut!

"We got her!" my mother exclaimed. "We got the mother and the kittens!"

"Now if we can just get Hunter to…," I said.

A blur of fur shot out of the wrecks—it was King! He charged across the clearing toward Hunter. Hunter leaped to the side as King, all fangs and fury, slammed into the cage holding Miss Mittens and the kittens, knocking it backward.

Hunter pounced on King. King screamed and jumped forward, trying to fight back, but Hunter had hit and run, leaping out of striking distance.

King scrambled forward, trying to get at Hunter.

"We have to do something!" I screamed. "We can't let him hurt Hunter or chase him away or—"

Hunter dashed around King and ran straight into one of the remaining traps. The door slammed shut, sealing him inside and King outside.

Dr. Reynolds jumped to his feet. In his hands was the snare pole. He ran toward King. As soon as King realized what was happening, he ran. Dr. Reynolds tried to grab him with the pole, but King was too far away and too fast. He vanished underneath one of the wrecks and was gone.

I should have been disappointed he'd gotten away. I wasn't. I was almost glad. Who needed him at the new colony? He was nothing but trouble, a bully, a...I felt guilty. Even King deserved to live. We still had time to catch him. Today, tomorrow or in a few days.

But I was too happy to feel bad or guilty about King. I was so grateful Hunter and Miss Mittens and all her kittens had been caught. Almost the whole colony had been caught.

I walked toward Hunter's cage, and then I saw somebody else—Rocky. The raccoon waddled across the clearing until he was beside Hunter's cage. He pressed his nose against it. Hunter did the same. The two animals touched noses through the bars of the cage.

"I wish I had a camera," my mother said.

"I wish I had another vet as a witness," Dr. Reynolds said.

"You don't need either. It's real. It's happening," I added. "Let's just watch."

"It looks like they're talking," Doris said.

They *are* talking, I thought. And I knew what they were talking about. They were saying goodbye.

I didn't need a witness to know this was real and that, when I told the story in a month, a year or fifty years from now to my grandchildren, it had happened. But still, I was glad to have four other people with me to watch it. Something special should be shared.

The two animals stood nose to nose, on opposite sides of the bars, one inside, the other out. It was real, but it wasn't. Maybe it *was* good I had some witnesses after all.

"Quickly! Quickly!" a voice yelled out. Mr. Singh came running into the clearing and the spell was broken. "You must leave!" he screamed. "You must leave! The police are coming!"

Twenty-Nine

We all froze. The only one who moved was Rocky. He waddled away, stopped for a second at the edge of the wrecks, looked back at Hunter, nodded and disappeared.

"You must all go!" Mr. Singh yelled again. "I will delay them as long as I can, but you must go, now!"

"Where are they?" Dr. Reynolds asked. "Are they at the front gate?"

"They are coming," Mr. Singh exclaimed. "I just got a call from them! They received a complaint, a call that somebody was in the junkyard, stealing, that there were intruders. They called to tell me, and they said they are sending somebody!"

"We have to leave, now," Dr. Reynolds exclaimed.

"That is what I am telling you," Mr. Singh yelled excitedly. "You must leave, quickly, so you are not caught!"

"Ladies, grab the empty traps," Dr. Reynolds ordered. "Simon, you get the snare poles. I'll take the mother and kittens, and Taylor, you better pick up Hunter."

We all sprang into action. I raced over to Hunter, trapped in his cage. He looked anxious and alert but not scared.

"It's going to be okay," I said. "You did the right thing. You saved everybody. Now we have to save us!"

I picked up the cage, and he edged away, rocking the cage, but I held firm.

There was a loud hiss as Dr. Reynolds picked up the other cage. Miss Mittens was hissing and snarling as she batted at the cage, trying to strike Dr. Reynolds's hands, desperate to defend her kittens.

"She'll be okay," I said to Hunter. "He won't hurt her."

Hunter let out a howl. It was so loud and plaintive it startled me. Miss Mittens's hissing continued, but she stopped trying to swat at Dr. Reynolds.

Doris and my mother had already reached the van and opened the back doors. The sound of the other cats was overwhelming. We loaded in the remaining empty cages, and Simon practically tossed the poles into the vehicle.

"Get in!" Dr. Reynolds yelled over the noise of the cats, and they raced for the doors. Dr. Reynolds loaded Miss Mittens in the back. "Give me the other one," he said.

I handed Hunter to him, and he started to put his cage on the other side of the van.

"No," I exclaimed. "He needs to be right beside her, where she can see him."

He didn't answer, but he did what I'd asked. He slammed the door closed and raced to the driver's door, while I ran to the other side and climbed in. My mother, Doris and Simon were hunched in the back, crammed among the cages.

"We made it," Doris said. "We made it."

"We would make it if I could find my keys," Dr. Reynolds said. He was trying to sound calm. "They can't be too far away," he said as he searched through his pockets. "There they are!"

He pulled them free, and the van roared to life. Dr. Reynolds pulled out of the junkyard and into the alley.

"We've made it!" Simon exclaimed. "And I won't have a criminal record to explain to my parents!"

"You better hold off on the celebration for a second," Dr. Reynolds said.

I looked out through the front windshield. A police car had turned into the alley and was coming toward us. It stopped directly in front of us, blocking our way. The doors opened, and two police officers got out.

"Let me do all the talking," Dr. Reynolds said.

That wasn't going to be a problem. I was too scared to think about speaking.

Dr. Reynolds rolled down his window as one officer came up beside him. The second officer stood off to the side.

"Good afternoon, officer," Dr. Reynolds said, trying his best to sound friendly and casual. "Is there a problem?"

The officer poked his head slightly into the van. "It certainly sounds like there's a problem in here. What have you got in here?"

"I'm a vet," Dr. Reynolds said. "Here's my id."

He pulled out a couple of pieces of ID from his wallet and handed them to the officer. He looked at them.

"And what are you and these people and these cats doing in this alley?" the officer asked. "How many cats are in there?"

"Quite a few," Dr. Reynolds said. "I am...I am transporting them, and these people are assisting me."

"And who is this boy?" the officer asked.

"He's my son!" my mother called from the back. "And I can give you some identification to show who I am as well."

"That would be good," he said.

My mother passed forward her identification, and he took that as well.

"Now, would somebody like to explain to me why you have...how many cats do you have in there?"

"About forty," I said without thinking.

"Thank you. Can somebody explain why you have forty cats in the back of this van?"

"As I was saying," Dr. Reynolds said, "I'm transporting these cats to my offices for an examination and treatment."

"Doc, I was born at night, but it wasn't last night," the officer said. "What I know is that there was a report of a white van parked where the fence had been broken and four or five people were inside the junkyard. Now here I am, standing beside a white van, the only white van I can see, and there are five people inside it. So once again, I'd like an answer."

"I've given you an answer," Dr. Reynolds said. "I'm sorry you don't like it, but that's my answer, unless you have proof of something different."

"Proof? You mean like going over there and taking casts of the shoeprints coming out of the yard and comparing them to your shoes? Do you mean that sort of proof?"

Dr. Reynolds swallowed hard.

"So would somebody like to tell me what you were doing in the yard?" he asked.

"We weren't doing anything wrong," I said. "Honestly."

"But you were in there, correct?"

"Yes, sir," I said.

He turned to Dr. Reynolds. "Now was that so hard? So what were you doing in there?"

"We were just—" Dr. Reynolds said.

"Not from you," he said. "I want to hear it from him. He hasn't lied to me, at least so far."

"We weren't taking anything, except for the cats."

"And why would you be taking these cats?" he demanded. He sounded angry.

"You don't understand," Dr. Reynolds said.

"Then let *him* explain," he said, pointing at me again.

"They're wild cats, feral cats, and we had to move them."

"And why is that?" he asked. He still sounded angry.

"Because of that," I said, pointing at a section of the fence that had a poster of the condos. "They're building condominiums, and the cats weren't going to have any place to live, if they even did live! They would have been killed during the construction!"

"And the owner of the property, the man who's developing this property, does he know all of this?" the officer asked.

"He doesn't know, and if he did, he wouldn't care," I said.

"So he doesn't know you're taking these cats?" he asked. "He didn't give you permission to take the cats or to be on his property, is that correct?"

I didn't want to answer, but I had to. "Yes, sir," I said quietly.

He let out a big sigh.

"But we had to do it!" I exclaimed. "We had to rescue them or they would have died. We had no choice, even if we didn't have permission!"

"And where are you bringing these cats to?" he asked.

"The Leslie Street Spit is gigantic," Dr. Reynolds said. "There are already two separate feral cat colonies out there, and there used to be a third."

The officer shook his head slowly.

"You have to know a couple of things about me," the policeman said. "First off, I've been a police officer for almost twenty years, and it is my sworn duty to uphold the law."

This was looking worse and worse.

"And, second, I have a cat named Pepper. He's a wonderful cat, almost a member of my family. So I'm going to back my car up, and you're going to drive away, right now, before any other squad cars arrive."

He handed the ids back to Dr. Reynolds and started to walk away, then spun around and came back to the van.

"And thanks for taking a chance. Sometimes you have to do what's right instead of what's strictly legal. Have a good day!"

Thirty

We drove slowly, very slowly, along the bumpy dirt road. It led out to a strip of land that jutted into the lake. There were bushes and trees all over and plenty of places where a cat could hide or hunt. I could see city office towers across the water, but where we were seemed more like a little piece of land up north, not the heart of Toronto.

Dr. Reynolds explained there was a connection between the land on which we were driving and those towers. The spit was created when the city had to find a place to dump the dirt it had dug up to build the foundations of those office towers. Somehow it seemed right that our cats, forced from their home by another tower going up, would make *this* land their home.

"There's lots of food out here for them to catch," Dr. Reynolds said.

"And people who come to feed them as well," Doris added.

"It is quiet here. There really aren't that many people who come out this way, although it seems busy today, especially for the winter," Dr. Reynolds said.

It wasn't city crowded, but there were more people than I would have expected. There were couples pushing strollers, people on bikes, joggers and people just out for a stroll. They created a steady stream of traffic. Dr. Reynolds said we should try to be inconspic-uous, but the sound of lots of cats calling out like they were being killed wasn't the best way to blend into the background.

It was getting close to nightfall. We probably had no more than an hour before sunset. Dr. Reynolds said we needed enough time and enough light to release the cats, but not so much light that we'd be seen. What we were doing wasn't really illegal, but it wasn't really legal either.

We'd repeatedly cruised past the spot where the colony was going to be reestablished. From the road, I could see a patchwork of partially buried concrete blocks, as well as some holes in the ground. It didn't look like much, but then again, neither did the junkyard.

"I think it's time," Dr. Reynolds said.

A chill went up my spine.

We waited for a couple of runners to jog past. They had earbuds in, so they weren't able to hear the cats.

Dr. Reynolds pulled the van over to the side, off the road and onto the gravel shoulder. He turned the engine off, and for a few seconds even the cats were silent, as if they knew something was about to happen. I knew *what* was going to happen, but I didn't know exactly *how* it was going to happen.

"We're going to have to do this all very quickly," Dr. Reynolds said. "From start to finish, we need to have all of this done and us gone within fifteen or twenty minutes."

"And if we take longer?" Simon asked.

"With each minute there's an ever-increasing risk somebody might call the police. We can't expect every officer to react like the last one."

"And what could they do?" my mother asked. "Would they charge us with something?"

"I don't even know what they could charge us with— littering maybe?" He laughed. "But still, we want to get this done quickly. Okay?"

"No arguments," I said. "Devon and his dad and the others are supposed to be here soon. Should we wait for them?"

"We don't have time to wait. If they come, great, but let's get started. We'll get the cages out and place them beside those cement blocks."

"Are there places for them to go? Nests, dens?" I asked.

"Plenty. This area used to hold a whole colony."

"What happened to those cats?" my mother asked.

"It might have been a disease, but it's been vacant for over two years. Whatever the problem was, it won't be a problem now," Dr. Reynolds said. "The junkyard cats are very healthy. I only wish I'd had time to examine and inoculate the last group of cats we captured."

There hadn't been any time. We'd come from the junkyard straight here. At least I knew Hunter was healthy.

"We're going to send somebody here every day for the next few weeks to feed them and help them settle in," Doris said. "The secret to reestablishing a colony is to give them massive quantities of food so they don't wander off, and to make sure the place is as contained as possible."

"You mean like with a fence?" I asked.

"Exactly. The whole spit is fenced in," Dr. Reynolds said. "And someone will be here every day to monitor the situation."

"Do you think I could come too?" I asked.

"It's pretty far from our apartment," my mother said.

"Not every day, but some of the times?" I pleaded.

"I'll drive you here some of the times myself," Dr. Reynolds said. "Now, enough talking, we have to get going. Aim the openings of the cages toward the holes in the ground. As soon as a trap is empty, bring it back into the van." He paused. "Once we get started, we just keep going, no stopping for anything. As soon as this next car passes, go. Get on your gloves."

We pulled on our heavy work gloves and watched as a little car approached, heading out of the park.

"Okay, go!"

We jumped out of the van. Dr. Reynolds threw open the back door and started handing out the cages. Doris took the first one, Simon the second, my mother grabbed the third and I took the fourth. I moved as fast as I could while carrying a cage with a crazed cat inside. The cat bounced against the bars.

"It's going to be okay, you're going to be fine," I said. "Just settle down and you'll be out in seconds."

I put the cage down beside a hole and fumbled with the latch. When I popped open the cage, the cat didn't seem to notice. It just sat there, not moving, not leaving. I didn't have time to wait. I raced back to the van as Simon and Doris and my mother put down their cages.

Dr. Reynolds had pulled a dozen cages out of the van onto the ground. I grabbed another cage, Sherpa's, and raced back to the new colony site. Simon was running toward the van, and I passed my mother and Doris, who were carrying an empty cage between them. Somebody had gotten out.

I kept moving. Sherpa hissed and snarled as I trudged forward.

"Give me a break!" I yelled at the cat.

I put the cage down and opened the door. Sherpa bounded toward a cement block and disappeared. I grabbed the empty cage and ran back to the van, passing the others running in the opposite direction. By the time I reached the vehicle, almost all the cages had been taken out and placed on the ground.

I had dropped my empty cage and went to grab another when I noticed we weren't alone. A car slowed down and pulled over.

"It's the guys!" I yelled.

Almost before the words were out of my mouth, the car doors opened and everybody jumped out! Without waiting for instructions, they grabbed cages and headed toward the new colony site.

"Sorry we weren't here earlier!" Devon exclaimed as they all ran toward us.

"Just glad you're here now!" Dr. Reynolds called out, and Devon dashed off.

I was grateful for the extra help. Now there were ten of us moving the cats toward freedom.

"Take this one," Dr. Reynolds said to me. He pulled the blanket off the cage, revealing Miss Mittens and her kittens.

"Sure, of course," I said.

"Then you come back for Hunter," Dr. Reynolds said, pointing to Hunter's cage.

Everything had been happening so fast I hadn't even thought about Hunter, but I did want to be the one to release him.

"Thanks!"

Dr. Reynolds grabbed a cage, and I picked up Miss Mittens. I tried to be gentle. The kittens were tucked underneath her, only partially visible. They were nursing. She looked scared, but she stayed down and allowed the kittens to continue to nurse.

"It's going to be okay," I said to her. "You'll have to carry the kittens out, but as soon as I put you down I'll go back and get Hunter. He'll help you."

At the release site there was a whole row of cages, some empty and some with cats cringing inside, too scared or confused to leave. I placed Miss Mittens's cage near the center and popped open her door. She didn't move.

"Here you go, Miss Mittens. You take care of those kittens," I said.

I picked up an empty cage and started back to the van. It was so much easier carrying an empty cage. I dropped the cage and went over to Hunter's.

He was standing, watching what was going on. He looked up at me and let out a meow, like he was asking, Where have you been and what are you waiting for?

"Sorry, I guess I should have gotten you first," I apologized. "You're the leader now, and I should have let you lead."

I carried him back to Miss Mittens and placed his cage right beside hers. Even though her cage was open, she hadn't left. She was still inside, nursing her kittens.

I went to open Hunter's cage and hesitated. I was going to come back and visit, but would he be here? Would I be able to find him? Was this the last time I was going to see him? The other cats had either remained in their cages or raced away like their tails were on fire. I didn't think Hunter was going to do either of those.

"Goodbye, Hunter," I said. "I'll see you again, but it won't be the same. You take care of yourself, and Miss Mittens and her kittens, *your* kittens. I'm going to miss you."

I opened up his cage. He walked through the opening and calmly looked around. He glanced up at me and walked directly into Miss Mittens's cage. I knew what would happen next.

The two cats touched noses, and then Hunter proceeded to pick up a kitten. He stepped out of the cage and tried to decide which way to go.

"Try any one of the holes," I suggested. "You can always move later if you don't like it. You're the leader now."

Hunter trotted over to a hole and looked in but didn't go down. It looked as if he was smelling the hole. He decided against that one and went to the next one, again, stopping at the top. This one must have been better, and he disappeared inside.

I knew I should have kept moving, carrying cats or empty cages, but I didn't. I couldn't leave. I needed to know what was going to happen.

I didn't have to wait long. Hunter came back out of the hole without the kitten. This was the new den. He headed straight for Miss Mittens's cage again.

He grabbed a second kitten, and Miss Mittens took the third. She followed him out of the cage, leaving one kitten behind. It cried pitifully. I had to fight the

urge to reach in, grab the little bundle of black fur
and take it over to the edge of the hole. I knew it was
important I didn't do that. I didn't want to leave my
scent on it.

I watched as Hunter and then Miss Mittens disappeared into the hole. I knew Hunter would be back soon
enough to get the last kitten.

There was a blur of movement all around me. The
last of the cages had been put down and cats were being
set free. Empty cages were being rushed back to the
van, and Dr. Reynolds was loading, practically tossing,
them in. A car had stopped beside our van, and there
were half a dozen people, on bikes and joggers, now
standing and watching us. No wonder Dr. Reynolds
was rushing.

Doris picked up a cage and gave it a little shake,
causing the cat inside it to tumble out.

"Sorry," she apologized as the cat scampered off.

She took the empty cage back to the van. Everybody
was hurrying, except for me. I couldn't help them until
Hunter came back for the last kitten. I looked over at
the hole. Why hadn't he come out? What was he doing?
The kitten continued to cry for its mother.

"Somebody will be back to get you soon, little one,"
I said. I turned back toward the hole. No Hunter. No
Miss Mittens. "Come on, Hunter, hurry up," I mumbled.

But he didn't appear.

"Everybody, hurry!" Dr. Reynolds yelled. "We have to leave soon!"

The pace got even faster. All around me, people were grabbing cages, rushing, hurrying. I felt guilty not working, but they were doing a great job without me. Almost all of the cats had escaped. Almost all of the cages had been returned to the van. I wasn't moving until the last kitten was retrieved. Come on, Hunter, hurry up. And then there he was—Hunter came out of the hole!

"Took you long enough," I called out. "What were you doing, remodeling?"

He ignored me and ran over to the cage, stepping partway inside to scoop up the last little kitten. He backed out of the cage. Now all he had to do was bring it down to Miss Mittens and the other kittens.

He started toward the hole but turned and came back toward me. What was he doing? He stopped in front of me, holding the kitten in his mouth. Was he saying goodbye? Was he trying to find a way without words to say to me what I wanted to say to him?

He gently placed the kitten on the ground. It started crying again and struggled to get to its feet. It was so young, it couldn't even stand, and there was something awkward about it.

Hunter looked up at me with his big eyes and let out a soft, gentle cry. I bent down so we were almost eye to eye.

"I'm going to miss you too," I said. "But this isn't goodbye. I'll be here sometimes, just not every day."

He gave another little cry.

"I know you'll take good care of everybody. You'll be a much better leader than King. You won't become a big, fat bully."

I sensed I wasn't alone. I looked over my shoulder. Everybody was standing behind me, a dozen feet away, watching. They were far enough away to give Hunter and me space, but close enough to hear me speaking to him. I didn't care.

"You better get going," I said.

Hunter picked up the little kitten.

"That's good."

He took a few more steps *toward* me until we were only a couple of feet apart. I reached over, slowly, carefully, and held out my hand. He rose up on his back feet and rubbed his head against my hand.

"The next time I come back, I'll give you a head scratch if you want," I said. "But you have to go. We *all* have to go."

"No rush," Dr. Reynolds said from behind me. "Take your time. I'm okay with being here a little longer."

"Yes," Doris said. "I just want to stand here and watch."

Hunter dropped onto all fours and set the kitten down on the ground again. He looked up at me, let out a soft little cry, then turned and walked away, leaving the kitten behind.

"Hunter, wait! What are you doing?" I cried out.

He kept walking, but he glanced over his shoulder.

"You've forgotten the kitten!" I called.

He turned away, moving faster until he came to the edge of the hole. He stopped, looked directly at me and disappeared inside.

I was shocked. What about the kitten? He couldn't have forgotten it. Open mouthed, I turned to Dr. Reynolds.

"The kitten...he didn't take the kitten," I stammered. "He forgot it."

"I don't think so," Dr. Reynolds said as he walked toward me. "He didn't forget it."

"He wouldn't just abandon it," I exclaimed.

"He didn't abandon it," Dr. Reynolds said. "He *gave* it to you."

"No," I said, shaking my head. "Why would he give me a kitten?"

The kitten was crying desperately for its mother. It struggled to get to its feet but couldn't seem to stand.

"Here," Dr. Reynolds said as he bent down and scooped up the little ball of black fluff. "Do you see that?" he asked.

I didn't see anything except a little black kitten.

"Look at this front paw," he said.

"What about the front…?"

Then I saw. The front paw, the right front paw, was *missing*. That's why it wasn't able to stand.

"That's why he gave the kitten to you," Dr. Reynolds said. "He knew it couldn't survive in the wild. He knew it *needed* you."

Dr. Reynolds handed me the kitten. It was so small, it weighed less than nothing.

"But we can't have a cat, can we?" I asked my mother.

"I think you already have a cat. Well, a kitten," she said. "But it's so small, so young, will we be able to care for it, feed it and raise it?"

"With our help, it can survive," Doris said. "It will need to be bottle-fed every few hours, and I can do the day shift until it's old enough to do without it."

"But what about the foot?" Simon asked. "Can a three-pawed cat survive?"

"I have a few three-legged cats in my practice. He couldn't survive in the wild, but he *can* survive as a house cat, and any medical treatment he needs, *forever*, is taken care of."

"That's so nice of you," my mother said.

"No, I insist. It's not every day you get to see a miracle happen," Dr. Reynolds said.

"What are you going to call him?" Simon asked.

I looked down at the little ball of fur in my hands—its eyes hardly open, crying out for its mother. Missing paw, black fur and there on its forehead was a little brush of white, just like his father.

"His name is Hunter," I said. "Just like his father." I smiled. "But I'll call him Junior so the two of them don't get confused."

"Now, we better get going. All of us, including your new kitten," Dr. Reynolds said.

He and Doris picked up the last two cages, and everybody headed back to the van. I looked back. Hunter was sitting at the edge of the hole. Our eyes met. He nodded his head, and I nodded mine.

"I'll look after him," I said.

He opened his mouth. I couldn't hear anything, but I knew what he said. "I know you will."

AUTHOR'S NOTE

Every Monday morning for ten weeks, students across the Toronto District School Board received twenty-six pages of a new, untitled manuscript. They each read a section, decided what they liked, what they didn't, what made sense and what they wanted changed. They would then email their feedback to me, and the book was edited and rewritten according to their suggestions. The title, *Catboy*, was one of the many suggestions that were incorporated into the final manuscript. While I am listed as the author, this book had hundreds of co-authors. Many thanks to the students of the TDSB for helping to make this book what it is today!

ERIC WALTERS began writing in 1993 as a way to entice his grade five students into becoming more interested in reading and writing. At the end of the year, one student suggested that he try to have his story published. Since that first creation, Eric has published nearly seventy novels. His novels have all become best-sellers and have won over eighty awards. Often his stories incorporate themes that reflect his background in education and social work and his commitment to humanitarian and social-justice issues. He is a tireless presenter, speaking to over 70,000 students per year in schools across the country. Eric lives in Mississauga, Ontario, with his wife and three children.

ERIC WALTERS

HUNTER

The story of *Catboy* told through very different eyes.

Hunter knows humans are dangerous to himself and the other cats of his colony. He avoids them, as all wild cats should. So when a neighborhood boy starts showing up in Hunter's junkyard to chase away dogs and bring the colony food, Hunter keeps his distance. But a new condo development puts the whole colony in danger, and Hunter soon realizes the only way to save his family is to put his trust in the boy.